Moon Dancer

Patrilla Elliott

A Strang Company

MOON DANCER by Patrilla Elliott
Published by Creation House Press
A Strang Company
600 Rinehart Road
Lake Mary, Florida 32746
www.creationhouse.com

This book or parts thereof may not be reproduced in any form, stored in a retrieval system, or transmitted in any form by any means—electronic, mechanical, photocopy, recording or otherwise—without prior written permission of the publisher, except as provided by United States of America copyright law.

Cover design by Terry Clifton

Cover art copyright © 2004 by Laura Crane

Copyright © 2004 by Patrilla Elliott
All rights reserved

Library of Congress Control Number: 2004102759
International Standard Book Number: 1-59185-565-9

04 05 06 07 08 — 9 8 7 6 5 4 3 2 1
Printed in the United States of America

For my father, Willie Keith Cotter, whom I love and miss.

And for my husband, Jay, who is the source of my earthly strength.

Acknowledgments

My most heartfelt thanks go to my mother for always believing in me.

My thanks and apologies go to my family and friends whom I greatly neglected while pressuring my dream. I appreciate the support.

Matt Davis, my son, for putting up with my insecurities and crying jags; also for the idea of my villain lady, Christina Emerald.

Tonya Vinyard, my daughter, for her support and belief in me. My three grandchildren, Eric, Robert, and Sara, I love you so much and our newest addition, Eric's little Jordan

Shelia Clemmons, a very dear friend. She is a rock I have leaned on many times over the past few years—late nights as well as long days spent in front of a computer, sometimes alone as well as with me. The most important contribution was, is, and always will be her belief in Moon Dancer and me. My thanks to her husband, Aaron, for sharing her with me.

Myrtle Hubbard Alexander, a wonderful lady who gave of her time and talent to objectively review Moon Dancer. Her endorsement and words of encouragement were greatly appreciated.

Carolyn White, owner of Autumn Harvest Inn, Williamstown, Vermont, for a wonderful week with her and her beautiful family. I went to do research and came away with new friends.

Adam Boyce, a local historian from Williamstown, Vermont, who opened the doors to the museum and took me on a tour providing me with much needed information, as well as becoming a new friend.

Contents

Preface	vi
The Inn in Vermont	1
Christmas Eve	17
The Room	31
The Journal	37
Judy—the Christmas Surprise	191
Christmas Morning at The Old Place	203
The Ride to the Orphanage	209
God's Little Angels	213
The Church	221

Preface

You hold in your hand a dream—one I thought would never to come to fruition. Being the daughter of a sharecropper and finding it hard to reach for an education, I thought realizing such a dream would be impossible. But life picked me up and made me travel on a tidal wave—marriage; a career; two beautiful children, Tonya and Matt; three grandchildren, Eric, Robert, and Sara; and one great-grandchild, Jordan.

One day the tidal wave miraculously slowed down and deposited me gently on shore. For the first time I was able to hear what life had been saying all along, "With God you can...with God you can just listen." When I did listen God answered my silent question with an equally silent answer. He gently laid this gift, *Moon Dancer*, in my flow of thoughts. It fell in rhythm with my life, becoming one with me. I listened to all and received this wonderful gift of love. Many emotional hours that turned into years are among these pages. I pray you will receive the silent gift and let it lay among your thoughts. Receive the messages as they blend with your flow of life. God most assuredly answers prayers. Just ask Abigail and me.

> Every good gift and every perfect gift is from above, and cometh down from the Father of lights, with whom is no variableness, neither shadow of turning.
>
> —JAMES 1:17

The Inn in Vermont

The pilot announced our arrival at the Burlington airport. I found it hard to believe that I was in Vermont. I had not been anywhere for years, not since my husband had died. For some time I had retreated to another place within myself. I was just now starting to make progress. My psychiatrist was encouraged and very much in favor of this trip. "You need to depend on yourself, Judy," he had said, "to find your inner strength, to see and experience the beauty of the world."

Frankly, I had my doubts until now. The first real excitement was starting to come over me. There is a rush one sometimes feels at the thought of the unknown. It is exciting and daunting. I had previously wanted to be alone with my grief, when I suddenly realized how vulnerable I had become. There was no protection, just my weakened self. I have come to believe this is when one starts to discover who he really is. I'm not sure, even now, if I'm ready to find the real me. I realized I do have to move on, let go of the past, and focus on the future, new places, people, and a new view on life.

After much searching, I settled on Williamstown, Vermont. I had fallen in love with its open beauty, fresh air, and its snow. How I loved the snow. I looked for an inn in Vermont that offered all of these things. "The Old Place" is its name. Located in the northeastern part of the state, it is accessible from any of the main cities and the capital, Montpelier. The inn is located in the rural farming area and has a fine history, distinctively of being one of the largest dairy farms in that area, and had been established in 1900 by Reginald and Eliza Duffin.

The Duffins were from England, the Isle of Man, which is located between the coast-line of England and Northern Ireland. They had inherited the farm from an uncle on the husband's side of the family. They took the chance, like so many others, for a new life in the New World. The farm had been added to over the years and now, as so many, had been converted to an inn.

I liked the romance of it all. The life of the place, having been around for so long, the snow, fireplaces, horses, and sleigh rides, but most of all I loved the big, old, beautiful three-story house. This had really excited me. I wanted to be on the top floor to see and experience all that was in and around The Old Place. I wanted to be alone with my thoughts, "just to wallow around," as my mother would say. This always brought a smile to my face. Her being such a beautiful woman, one would have a hard time envisioning her doing so. But, being as down to earth as she was, she obviously did. There was the real reason for my smile.

The opening of the door to the plane brought me back to reality. As we were walking from the plane I

The Inn in Vermont

stopped to survey my surroundings. There was a van parked by the entrance to the small airport with "The Old Place" written on the door. Taking a deep breath I made a commitment to live again, to let go of the past, to get caught up in the present as well as the future. With this decided, I walked toward the young man waiting beside the van.

He introduced himself as Chris. He said he would be taking me to the farm just outside of Williamstown. There, I would be met by one of the staff named Buck. The other guests and I would be taken by sleigh to The Old Place.

The ride was pleasant and very beautiful. It was Christmas time. The houses were lending a festive show to the season. Christmas has always been my favorite time of the year. It was only midmorning; the snow on the ground lay undisturbed and so beautiful. It seemed only a short while later that Chris pulled into the drive of a rather large barn with outbuildings. He smiled, "There's your ride. Looks like there are only two others who will be with you." There was an elderly lady and a somewhat younger man standing by a beautiful red sleigh trimmed with silver bells. The bells continued on up the reins to the most magnificent horses I had ever seen. I could feel the child in me start to awaken.

The cold morning air was invigorating as I stepped from the van. Chris loaded my luggage into the back of an old pickup truck. He walked back to me and said, "Sam will be taking the luggage on to the house. He has been with us for many years. Enjoy your stay, and have a merry Christmas." I thanked him and wished him the same. As I was walking toward the couple, I suddenly stopped, and my breath caught in my throat. The largest man I had ever seen appeared from behind the horses. He was checking the harness and sleigh. He was handsome, in a rugged way. I smiled when I realized I was also thinking of him as balanced. One doesn't usually think of a handsome man as balanced, but even with his size he was graceful. His rugged face had a gentleness about it, and his large hands touched the horses with softness. But he wasn't just at work; he was enjoying his work. Yes, balanced was appropriate.

His eyes twinkled, and his face lit with laughter as he helped the elderly lady and her companion into the sleigh. Suddenly, he was walking toward me with an outstretched hand. "My name is Buck," he said. "You must be Judy. May I call you Judy?" I answered, "Yes, please. It's nice to meet you, Buck." "We will all become as family for a while. It's less formal. How was your trip?" he asked. I answered, "Very well, thank you. The view from the air was just beautiful." After introducing me to Mrs. Peoples and her son Patrick, Buck helped me into the sleigh, and we were on our way.

The ride was full of small talk about everything and nothing. I answered only when politeness demanded I do so. I was caught up in the beauty of my surroundings. The bells on the sleigh were rhythmic. I could hear and feel the crunching of the snow as the sleigh moved slowly along. A relaxed, sleepy feeling came over me. Just as I was about to give in, I caught sight of the house.

The Inn in Vermont

It was even more breathtaking than the picture, and I loved it immediately. There were many windows and a large porch that went around the house. A large barn was to its left and in front of it, just to its right, was a very huge old tree. There was something under it, but we were too far away for me to make it out. A warm peace started to come over me. I thought how strange I felt, like I was coming home. It had been a long time since any place felt like home.

I couldn't wait to see inside the house. What great fun to explore this beautiful old place. A very tiny older lady greeted us at the door. Buck introduced her. "This is Miss Minnie. She has been here even longer than the house," he added. She made a playful sign of protest by pushing him out of the house, and he left with a hearty laugh ringing in the air.

There were others about, talking and settling in, but Miss Minnie turned to me with a smile. "You must be Judy, the young lady who wanted a wallowing room," she said laughing. I answered, "Yes, you remembered." As she led the way up the stairs I heard her say, "Even at my age I don't forget very much."

Miss Minnie held the door to my room open for me. She said, "A room away from the traffic of the house. A Victorian, cozy fireplace, very big windows, with lots of snow." We entered the room, and she gestured toward the bed. There were lots of pillows. She said, "Welcome to the attic room, Judy. You are the only one on this floor." I was overwhelmed. Everything was there, exactly what I asked for. It was as I pictured it. "What a wonderful surprise, thank you." " So you like surprises," she said. "Oh, yes, as long as they are nice ones," I answered, looking into the face of this tiny little lady. She said to me with a smile and a twinkle in her eye, "You will receive many surprises while you are here, but never a bad one."

Miss Minnie walked across the room, opened the door, and said, "I have drawn a bath for you. I thought you would like to change and rest for a while. Would you like tea and a sandwich now?" I answered, "Tea, now, and one of your surprises in my room would be nice. Thank you." She closed the door so quietly with no sound from the hall. It was as though no one had been there. What an interesting lady. She was obviously in her late eighties, but very active.

The bathroom was as one would expect in an older house. It had a footed tub with a narrow, high basin and, for beauty and comfort, a Victorian armchair. There was a vanity and the most exquisite large mirror. By the bathtub on a small table was a glass of wine and a small, floral china plate that held two plump figs.

After the wine and figs, which I enjoyed, I soaked in the warm water. I closed my eyes and must have dozed, for I did not hear Miss Minnie as she quietly entered the room placing some of my personal items about. I awoke thinking I must be in a dream, which, in these surroundings, was a dream within a dream. Forcing myself back to reality, in this house and these rooms, was not an easy thing to do. I had another surprise on the vanity where all my toiletry items were. There was makeup and a small, soft green china bud vase holding one perfect yellow rose. Leaning next to the vase was a small card signed *MM*. I smiled to myself. When and how did she do all this? I had not heard a sound.

The Inn in Vermont

As I entered my bedroom, with the soft glow of firelight warming the many antiques about, I noticed a wonderful old glider rocker by the hearth. All of my books were close enough for me to reach. My clothes had been put away, along with my luggage. Everything looked and felt like home. It was then I noticed a tray that held a beautiful Victorian tea set and a small plate with two finger sandwiches. Reaching for the teapot, I saw the small card with *MM*. How could she do these things? I never knew she was there.

That had to have been the best tea and sandwiches ever. As I sat for a while watching the shadows play on the wall and listening to the crackle of the fire, I dozed off. When I awoke, there before me was a lovely light supper on a place setting matching the tea service. I couldn't remember ever feeling so loved, warm, and taken care of in my life—and I had only been here a few hours.

How do you explain comfort, or the way a room wraps its way around you? How you are one with the coziness of the fire? Nothing else is there, only the blending of this one space and time, you so belong. You and it have always been, no words for it. For some time I walked the corridors of my mind letting the fire and the room take me back to another place and time. The shadows had deepened as the time passed. I rose and walked to the window and stood in awe, so stunned by the beauty before me, but at the same time feeling I had always known it was, that it had always been here.

A full moon cast its soft light over the snowbound trees and the grounds below. No picture would ever bring to life the splendor of what I saw. It would be an injustice to even try. Somehow I had the feeling that what I saw was just for me. I thought if I looked close enough I would see a small card signed *MM* somewhere out there in all that beauty. The rest of the night was a blur. I would wake only slightly, just enough to feel the room and the pillows. I felt as though I were sleeping on a cloud. Then the room would lull me back to sleep.

The dawn broke, bringing with it what some would have thought was a bad day. To me, it was perfect. How I loved the blowing snow and the howling of the wind around the eaves of the attic room, perched high atop this lovely old home. I felt cradled and cared for. I'm not sure how long I stood there by the window and watched the white world around me, so mesmerized I almost didn't hear Miss Minnie as she entered the room. It was then I realized that sometime during the night the dishes had been cleared away. The most amazing thing was how at peace I was with these strangers. They didn't feel like strangers at all. I didn't feel upset at them for moving about as I slept. I was feeling content and comfortable at the thought of them doing so. I was slowly changing.

At Miss Minnie's "Good afternoon, Judy," I turned with a startle. Afternoon? How long had I slept, or was it, how long had I gazed at the wonderland surrounding me? She laughed at the look on my face and answered the unspoken question there, "Yes, you, princess, in your bell tower, almost slept the clock around, and you look beautiful for your rest. I've brought you hot cocoa and finger foods. I'm sure you will want to join everyone later for our lovely Christmas Eve dinner. The meal is always wonderful and the evening so magical. You haven't seen The Old Place in all its splendor." I asked, "Would you

The Inn in Vermont

tell me about The Old Place, its history and its people?" She answered, "Now, you never mind, young lady; eat your food. Change into climbing around-the-house clothes, and I'll see you get your tour and history lesson." I thanked her for the lunch and assured her I would be waiting. My mind began to move with so many imagined answers to all the questions I had.

When Miss Minnie returned I was ready. She laughed at my baggy clothes and piled high fluffy hair that bounced around as I moved. I said, as I twirled around, "These are my Old Place getting-to-know-you clothes." As we walked down the hall, she said, "Most people want to get to know a house from the bottom up. They start in the most beautiful rooms, but you, my dear, started from the top. This floor is not open to guests, but there was something in your voice when we spoke on the telephone that made me think you needed the solitude. Now I can see you want to go straight to the heart of The Old Place. It's here," she said as she opened the door to a room. I can only describe it as one filled with love. Everywhere in the huge room was a lifetime of things well loved. They were loved too much to sell or give away, one treasure after another. As I moved around the room in wonder, I looked at Miss Minnie. She smiled and went back to the door. She said, "You don't need me to do the telling; the answers are here, my dear, here in this room."

Miss Minnie closed the door gently, and I was left alone with the whole of someone's lifetime. Lamps glowed softly all around the room. There were chairs of every shape and size, desks, boxes, stools, everything imaginable and from so many periods of time, so many years. I laughed with glee at the mountain of pillows and cushions about the floor. I piled them one on another and climbed in the middle as I went through an old trunk.

So many pictures in beautiful old family albums all stacked away and forgotten. These people had all been born, lived, loved, and died; they had a life. Now their likeness and essence were in this room, in an old trunk. For some unknown reason I wasn't sad for them, those who were no more. They had been here in and around this old place. In this world they had lived their life. Somehow, I felt they were satisfied. So strange, how I could feel comfort and peace from them and The Old Place.

I lost track of time as I became so engrossed and enchanted with the people and the life of this old place. There were so many letters over many periods of time. I became caught up in the lives of people who had been from almost every profession, so very interesting. Some had shared their happiness as well as their sorrows. I could relate to some and even gain help and solace. No matter the time we live in, each of us experiences what life has to offer, be it positive or negative.

For the first time I noticed the shadows were growing deeper and that darkness was starting to cover the windows. I thought I should feel rushed with the big Christmas Eve dinner almost upon me. I found I was at ease, as though somehow I knew they wouldn't start without me. It was then I noticed a big, beautiful, old Bible with a rich mahogany cover. It had gold lettering, made even more beautiful and soft by the many years of loving hands. When I opened it, I found it was a Bible that contained a family tree complete with

The Inn in Vermont

pictures. Someone had invested much love and time on these pages. To be a Bible as well-used as this one spoke volumes about the family. Such a shame for it to be here, locked away where so few could see and appreciate it. Then I realized it was of no importance to others, only to those who lived the pages and the pictures that were their life.

I felt blessed to be able to see, if only a small glance, what must be a special gift. A life will be lived and full with the Bible at the heart of it. There were so many children born. There were so many members to pass away in their due time with such long lives so well spent. There were doctors, lawyers, ministers, and just simply Christian people of all walks of life, a life well lived. So much peace I was feeling. What a wonderful way to spend a stormy winter day of blowing snow, here in the attic, the heart of an old home filled with a lifetime of living and love. My mind wandered away for a time among the shadows and memories. When I moved to put away the Bible, a small card fell to the floor. Picking it up, I wasn't surprised to see, and smiled, at the letters *MM*. How did she know the very thing that would make me happy, as well as the very things I needed? I could feel myself growing stronger among these memories. I was starting to come to terms with life through my experience with this room. I couldn't help thinking that Miss Minnie was a very perceptive lady who had learned many of life's lessons. She was truly a jewel, and The Old Place was fortunate to have her.

I was startled back to the present as the door opened and Buck seemed to fill the room. I had only seen him on the outside, and I knew he was a big man, but even in the vastness of the attic his size was pronounced. I smiled to myself for thinking of him as an outside man. Inside he would be filling doorways as he was now doing. I wondered if he was always bumping into things and tripping over rugs. When I came to myself, he was smiling as if he knew where my mind had wandered. His eyes were smiling as well. I had not realized how vibrant and blue they were. I had to look away to keep from staring. He said, "Miss Minnie said I would find you here. How was your day?" he asked. I answered, "Just beautiful. I can't remember when I have enjoyed a day more. Most people hate stormy days with so much snow. There is beauty in most everything, if we only look," I finished. He spoke so softly that I almost didn't hear his reply. "Yes, there is so much beauty." I'm not sure how long we were transfixed by the sheer force of ourselves. A noise from somewhere in the house brought us back. He smiled, laughed nervously, and said, "Dinner is in an hour." I answered, "Thank you, I'll see you downstairs." I was very surprised reacting toward him in that manner. Before, another man would have never crossed my mind. It was as if I was waking from a long sleep. Strange, this thing called human nature. How do you put away the past and return to the present? How could I leave this place that had a familiar feel and was full of love, where I was free to be myself, with my own thoughts? I didn't want to be in a room with strangers and make small talk, but good manners wouldn't allow me to do otherwise.

The Inn in Vermont

I descended the stairs in my one claim of a party dress I had brought with me. It was a floor-length, emerald green velvet with long sleeves. I was comfortable with myself; to further ensure this, I let most of my strawberry blond hair lie about my shoulders, with the rest piled softly on my head. Now mind you, I'm not a young girl anymore, but not old by any means. I'm a woman. I decided, *This is just what I will be tonight, a woman. I'll stay somewhere in the middle, not too much a part of the room and not so little as to be rude.*

Halfway down the stairs, a glimmer caught my eye. I turned my head, and there was a large set of doors through which I could see a large fireplace with flames dancing about, making wonderful soft shadows on everything in the room. The most commanding thing in the great room was the Christmas tree. It stood at least eight feet high with candles on every branch. The scent of pine was ever so soft. I thought I had never seen a tree more beautiful. The spirit of Christmas filled the room.

There was a large Queen Anne armchair covered with a rich floral tapestry. I was almost afraid to sit, but it was so inviting. I sat and drank in the beauty of the tree, the fire, and the very essence of the room. I noticed so many fine antiques. They were the type that had been used and loved with the passage of time. Not just show pieces, their years of use only added to their beauty. I found I was to, once again, marvel at how much I was feeling and experiencing life and my surroundings since my arrival here. To feel. It is so natural and at the same time

Moon Dancer

I would not be able to explain it, if I were asked. The smallest amount of my feelings was ever so much out of my comprehension. My mind went to the others I was to meet. I could feel myself pull away. How selfish of me, I thought. I had been given an opportunity to know the upper part of the house, its heart, as Miss Minnie had called it. To enjoy this room and get to know The Old Place on my own, with the peace that comes from one's self. Now, I was to begrudge a few hours I'm to share with warm loving people.

Why had the family opened their home? Had they fallen on hard times, or did they just enjoy having people around? It is rather a large place. Lots of outbuildings, a small dairy still remains, not as big as before, this I had been told. Why had I not met the owner? Who were they? How lucky for us, myself and others, to have a chance to spend Christmas in Vermont. Complete with snow, mountains, horse-drawn sleigh, warm hospitality, and this room with the dancing firelight. I rose and walked to the hearth to feel the warmth of the fire. When I placed my hand on the mantle, I saw the small card with *MM*. Miss Minnie and her surprises; she was as good as her word. I was amazed at how easily she pulled one after another. Perhaps she went about leaving cards in only the most interesting places. Was she really setting them all up, or was I just finding what she left for any one of us to find? She was either a very clever lady or just having fun with us, maybe both.

Warm smells were working their way around the room with soft sounds of laughter and music. I was about to leave the room when I noticed the tree had small gold cards on leach limb. I took one and read it, realizing it

The Inn in Vermont

was the tree Miss Minnie had spoken of earlier. Each of the guests, as well as the staff, was to choose the name of a child to buy a gift for Christmas. Such a wonderful feeling, when you can help make Christmas special for someone else, especially a child. I tucked the card inside a small pocket on my dress, smiling to myself. I left the room following the smells and sound of Christmas Eve dinner in The Old Place.

Christmas Eve

As the evening progressed I began to feel both apart from and a part of the evening. It was strange to feel that everything went on without me and also existed because of me. I found it wasn't too difficult, after all, to be there. I didn't have to do anything, just be natural.

There were the usual guests, the kind of people who want to get away for a while. Then there were the romantics, like me, who love the romance of time and place and try to relive what once was. I wanted to experience a small piece of time gone by, to live the fairytale. Warm my heart enough to live in this, the present.

Mrs. Peoples and her son Patrick were the only ones I had met. They were from Boston. There they were living their lives, going in different directions: she growing older, and he not wanting to see her do so. They appeased themselves with a few days each year at The Old Place. Barbara and Steven Conner, newlyweds, which is an explanation in itself. There were two elderly ladies, Miss Marie and Miss Nancy, without any close relatives. They each had a little money and chose to travel, sharing the lives of those they met along the way. Really, they are very likeable ladies, even for their eccentricities. Then there was myself, who just needed to regroup and get reacquainted with who I am. Being ill for so long had really taken its toll on me.

Sitting with the others and listening to the laughter and chatter, I realized I was listening to the house as well. Sounds were coming from all around. There was a hushed conversation and a deep male laugh, which seemed to come from back behind the dining room. No one noticed as I slipped out of my chair to follow the sounds. Coming to a large door, I pushed, and surprisingly, it opened with ease. I had to put my hand over my mouth to keep a gasp from being heard. I had truly moved back in time. The most wonderful old kitchen I had ever seen was before me. It had a large open-hearth fireplace with hooks and hangers of all sizes. There were steps, three levels high, and at the bottom, the stone hearth came out at least six feet. Lying on the hearth were two rather large sleeping dogs. One raised his head slightly, then went back to sleep. To the right of the fireplace were large wall racks filled with hanging coats and scarves. Shoes were all lined in a row under the coats. Another door, identical to the one I had just entered, was just a little to its right. A large window was over a workspace of old wooden tables. The windows were covered with shutters that had been closed to protect the glass from the wind and blowing snow, which could be heard from outside. A soft howling sound was made as the wind blew around the eaves. At the very back of the room was the very reason for its existence, a very large

Christmas Eve

stove that covered most of that section. I could tell it was old and had been here for many lifetimes. It was a wood-burning stove. The faint smell of it mingled with the fireplace and the pleasing aroma of the Christmas dinner. It was covered with pots and pans of all shapes and sizes. Metal racks were hung everywhere to accommodate them. Soft candlelight illuminated a most unique feature, one I truly loved and found fascinating. The outside wall and back were of solid stone. I was not sure what kind of stone, but I would ask someone later. For all the magic the room possessed, I was once again drawn to my favorite, the fireplace with its magical dancing fire.

For a while I wasn't noticed. Buck and an older man were playing checkers. Buck had a soft laugh with a chuckling sound. This was whom I had heard from the dining room. His eyes were twinkling as he teased his opponent, greatly enjoying every minute. He caught my eye, gave me a huge smile, and winked as though to say, "You just watch me, I'll get Pops yet."

I was surprised to see that there wasn't anyone else in the kitchen, with all the cooking going on and guests at the table. Miss Minnie appeared at that moment from the back of the room, with a smile that was almost too big for such a little lady. She came up to me, tied an apron around my waist, and said, "Now, you get to work, young lady. We have a dinner to serve." She handed me a rather large platter and, holding the door open, motioned me through. As I stood there, startled, Buck let out a laugh and threw me another wink. The next few hours were a flurry of activity. Forgotten were my fears and need to be alone. I soon discovered I was getting to know yet another room in The Old Place as well as one within myself.

Moon Dancer

As everyone drifted off to bed, the sounds in the house were fewer. The dining room seemed empty now. The fire was banked; embers glowed dimly as the once roaring fire slowly died out. As I stood watching, I found I was equating it to life. We burn brightly for a while, and later on we enjoy being the embers, not burning too brightly, but still very much alive. I was analyzing myself and found that I needed to think and sort through the corners of my mind.

When I took the last of the trays to the kitchen, I thought how different it was now with the fire low and the kitchen cleaned. I put away the last of the dishes myself. The sisters, Martha and Bernadette, had already left for home and their families as soon as the meal had been prepared. Miss Minnie told me they had grown up in service to others and had been with the Hastings since they were in their teens.

I sat down in front of the fire and was thankful that most of the lights had been turned out. The light from the fire was warm and calming. It was then I realized I was sitting in the same chair Buck had been in before dinner. I thought I could still feel him there. If I turned my head just so, I could hear his laughter and see the twinkle in his eyes. How strange for this man to slowly overtake my thoughts. The more I passed him over in my mind, preferring to wonder about The Old Place and the early years, the more he became entwined in the very presence of The Old Place, as though he was somehow in the fibers connected to me. I couldn't explain

Christmas Eve

my attraction to him. I don't react to strangers this way, but, again, he didn't feel like a stranger. I'm not sure how long I sat, lost in my thoughts, when I heard a faint rustling sound. I looked up to see Miss Minnie at the back of the room. When I stood up, a small card fell to the floor, I stooped, picked it up, and pointed it at her, and we both laughed. She motioned for me to follow her. As I did, I said, "I wonder which one you will run out of first, cards or surprises." She smiled and opened a small door that concealed a flight of stairs.

She proceeded up. I followed with excitement and a feeling I was at a loss to explain. This and the kitchen were like old friends, someone I knew well and found so peaceful.

Up the stairway we went. The stairs were very small, but not for Miss Minnie. I asked, "Were these made for you?" She answered, laughing, "They were built to be secret. The old manor houses of this size and larger had them built for the servants to take care of the master and mistress, as well as the guests, without being seen. The Old Place wasn't big in the beginning. It was added onto over the years. That is when the stairs were put in. They are much quicker and a lot warmer to use in winter, rather than having to cross the whole of the house to get to the main stairways. I heard some were used for late night liaisons, but these things were never thought of here. This is a home with faith at its core, and if at all possible, they would have used angels as corner support beams instead of stone." This she said stopping on the stairs with a tight stance and firm nod of the head, as if to say, "And that is the end of that."

We climbed in the partial darkness. This we did in

silence. We came to a small landing to the right of the stairs. I could see more clearly. There was attached to the wall a small light. The sconce was of scrolled brass, with a delicate, fluted glass globe. I thought it was too beautiful to be hidden away here, where only a few could see.

Miss Minnie gently pushed on a small square of a cutout resembling a door without a knob. It soundlessly opened. I gasped as we stepped into my room. I turned and watched as the wall become whole again. There was not a trace of where we had entered. I said in surprise, "This is how you have been coming and going from my room, as if by magic. I was beginning to think you were a ghost or a little fairy." She laughed and said, "Some mystery is fun and should be enjoyed to the limit. You needed the magic, especially when you first arrived." I asked, "How are you so perceptive? None of you have ever met me, but you read my likes and dislikes so very well." She answered, "Some people are testaments unto themselves. They bring their persona with them as they would wear an outer garment, very visible for those of us who are willing to take the time to notice; this I did." At that moment, I experienced a strong bonding with Miss Minnie, and I was sure she would be very prominent in my future.

I walked back to the wall and asked, "How do you open the door from this side?" She walked over to a wall sconce that held a flickering candle, reached up, and pushed the bottom gently. The wall opened without a sound. It was exciting and a little scary. While I was marveling at how this was accomplished and at my acceptance of it, Miss Minnie had sat in a chair by the

Christmas Eve

fireplace. The chair seemed to swallow her small frame. I had visions of Alice in Wonderland. She motioned for me to sit as she said, "You and I will have tea. We have a lot of talking to do. I can see questions all over that pretty face of yours." "Yes," I said. "My first one is, when did you get the preparations for such an elaborate tea as this up here?" She gave me a knowing smile and said, "I brought it up by the stairs while you were dreaming by the kitchen fire. You looked like you needed some time alone." I was pondering this when it came to me, and I asked, "How did you make tea without my hearing you?" She answered, "Oh, I get lost in the vastness of this place. Sounds are greatly minimized."

I wasn't sure if I understood her answer or my reaction to it. As I sat in the chair across from her, I decided to put that question away until another time. I settled myself comfortably as I watched the flames dancing from the fire. That was one of the things I loved about The Old Place, all of the fireplaces. I'm sure there was one in every room, at least every one I had been in. The room became so cozy. I could feel it close around me. As Miss Minnie began to talk she seemed to be eight, eighteen, and eighty, all at the same time, switching back and forth in time as she talked into the night. At one moment she said, "I'm not sure which came first, me or The Old Place." I had the feeling that they were one and the same. One could not exist without the other.

We talked of the family and the Christmases of long ago, the many years past, other families, and the wonderful times they had here. On Christmas morning they would gather from far and near, assemble in the large front drawing room downstairs, the one with the big Christmas tree of lights. There they would share a big breakfast and open presents before going on a sleigh ride into town. They would visit the orphanage, which was the love and life of the Hastings family. When I looked at her, there was sadness upon her face. This was new. I had not seen this before. I asked, "Where are they this Christmas, Miss Minnie? Why aren't they here?" "They, my dear, is really just one: Abigail. She is the only one left of the family and myself. I exist for her, only her. The people you are speaking of, the ones you saw in the albums, are exactly where they are supposed to be, with their families, living their lives. They have a purpose now, because of one woman, a great lady, who now lies in a hospital, waiting for her time to be with God and the love of her life, Carl. I see the puzzled look on your face, so I will tell you of her life, so you will understand."

I poured us a fresh cup of tea. I could see she needed time to gather her thoughts. This was very close to her. When I had settled again, I sipped my tea and waited for her to begin her story. "Reginald Duffin and his wife, Eliza, came from England to Vermont in 1899, bringing with them a baby girl, Abigail. They had inherited this place from Reginald's uncle on his mother's side and decided to make a life in this New World.

"The original house was built about 1869. It was small by today's standards, but just right for their small family. When Abigail was ten, there was a fire. Most of the house was consumed before the fire could be contained. Abigail was trapped in the back part, behind the kitchen. This was her favorite place to play, and the kitchen, how she loved that kitchen. She was always fascinated by the stone walls, which make up the outside and back walls.

Christmas Eve

It was some time before they realized she was there. A beam had struck her on the head and shoulder. She had inhaled smoke as well. In time she recovered, but the memory always stayed with her. They rebuilt the house in the same place leaving the stone walls of the kitchen, which have been a great source of enjoyment for all of us over the years." She looked at me and smiled when she said this. I'm not sure, but I think I may have blushed, for I was remembering what I had been thinking at the time. She paused and began again, "She would never think of leaving this place. It has been her life. Everything she is and ever was is wrapped up in this place.

"When she turned twelve, she met Carl, her husband. He was seventeen and quite a good-looking young man. The first time she had seen him was in town. She was with her mother. When Carl had passed, she asked who he was. Her mother had replied that he was Mr. Master Hastings' son. She was confused, for his farm was the closest one to theirs and she had never heard of or seen him. When she said this to her mother, her mother replied that Carl had been away at school. His father had big plans for him. She said, 'That young man will make something of himself. His father will see to that.'

"As fate would have it, on one of Abigail's outings, which was most always to Sutters Pond, for she loved that pond, she had gone to her spot on a bluff. She could see well all around. There he sat in her spot. She walked right up to him and introduced herself without hesitation. She was always one to make her own mind. She never let anyone elicit rules on her life. She always had spunk and at ninety-one still does." When she said this, my head had sprung up. I said, "She is ninety-one. Didn't you say earlier that you were older than she is?" "Yes, dear, I did. I am ninety-three years old. Strange, isn't it, that life can deal with each of us differently." I replied, "You truly must have been happy. I would never have guessed your age." She smiled. As she sat in silence, a faraway look came upon her face. I waited for a few minutes before I asked, "Miss Minnie, will you tell me about Carl?" She paused a moment to gather her thoughts, then said, "After that day, whenever Carl was home, he would always meet Abigail at Sutters Pond. He told her that his father was very strict and would stop them from seeing each other if he found out. He wanted Carl to enter a life of politics. He said it wasn't just Abby; it would be anyone. Poor Carl, he so wanted to live a quiet life here in this beautiful state. His dream was to have his own place with a lumber business, a large dairy, and to become a veterinarian. His life. It may not have been too glamorous, but it was still his life. But old Master Hastings would not have it. His son was going to be somebody and go as far as he could push him. He said that no son of his was going to move down in his station in life."

A few moments went by. She continued, "One day when Abigail was fourteen, almost fifteen, her world changed. She had known for some time that she had feelings for Carl, and she was sure he felt the same way, though no words were spoken. She was waiting for him at their special place at the pond. When he arrived, he was very upset. He said his father had arranged a marriage between him and the daughter of a prominent attorney from Montpelier. This man was running for the senate and of course would see to it that his son-in-law would follow in his footsteps. They were both devastated. Carl

Christmas Eve

had tried to get his father to change his mind. He said plans had been made and that was the end of the discussion. Carl left that following Christmas. He said good-bye to Abigail and just disappeared.

"His father searched for a year and finally just gave up. He became a very bitter old man. Poor Abigail, she just moved from one day to the next. The years passed; she never would see any of the other young men in town. She was pretty and was asked, but she just did not have a heart. Carl had taken it with him. She chose to get an education; she would not leave home. She attended local schools and college. She knew almost as much as her father did. Many times she would do the payroll, as well as buying and selling. Mr. Reginald was a good man with his own way of thinking. To him, it was fit and proper for his daughter to be educated and help with the farm. The men of the town in those days, however, did not take too kindly to women being educated. They believed it was a waste of time and money.

"No one knew about her and Carl, so she grieved alone." I had sat quietly, listening as Miss Minnie talked, trying to put myself in the place of this young girl of so long ago. How her heart must have ached, as mine had when I lost Paul. I had to stop the old pain, before it took over.

Miss Minnie asked, "Are you all right, dear?" "Yes, I am fine," I answered. "Please go on." She sighed as she leaned back against the old chair that so engulfed her. Staring into the fire she began to speak, "This, my dear, is when I entered their lives and they totally became mine.

"My mother was in charge of the Walden house, just outside of East Barer, in Chittenden County. I had grown up there and was educated by my mother and others in her service. Mother heard that Eliza Duffin was in need of someone to care for her home.

"She thought I should apply for the position. My age could have been a problem, if not for my credentials, and since this was a small household, at the time, they most likely would overlook that one minor flaw. You see, I was seventeen. My age was right, for Abigail and I in time became friends. I shall never forget the time, so long ago, when two very different young ladies forged a bond that would last a lifetime.

"We were having tea by the fire; when she began to pour, I insisted it was my place to do so. I reminded her that she was, after all, the lady of the house. She looked straight at me and said, 'I can and will pour for you, and I will serve you a meal, as well as you can for me. Secondly, there are two ladies in this house.' From that day to this she has had my loyalty, gratitude, and love. I know, Miss, I can see that question on your face, and the answer is no. She did not tell me about Carl. She confided in me after their marriage, but I am getting ahead of myself." She became quiet; there was sadness about her. After a few minutes she said, "It is late, and I want to share with you the night before she was taken to the hospital. I will tell you the rest of what I was telling you tomorrow, on the way to the orphanage.

"Abigail and I were enjoying the fire and sipping hot cocoa. She was very quiet. I asked, 'Why so quiet?

Christmas Eve

You seem to have something on your mind.' She put her cup down, turned to me, and said, `Yes, Minnie, I am ready to go home. My work here is finished. I am finally ready. I had a wonderful life, filled with so many moments that I treasured. I believe they will dwell on, in my spirit, after I am gone, so many blessings. All I ask God for is just to take me home. I want to be with Him and those I love who are waiting for me. I know my precious Carl is waiting. I feel him, Minnie, more this past year than since he has gone. Every day his presence becomes stronger. I feel he is slowly wrapping himself around me, like I am in a cocoon. I feel so protected, Minnie. For some time now the faces of my parents have become faded. I still remember them; they are just very dim. Now, I see them, just as they were on the fateful day so long ago. No, please, you don't have to respond.' She took my hand and said. `You my dear Minnie, have been a true and loyal friend and sister. I should never have survived without you. Thank you for your love and friendship. We discovered its true meaning, didn't we? It is not about perfection, but effort, to see the true quality of a person. I believe we accomplished this. I will be waiting for you. We will embark on a new and wondrous journey in God's house. My earthly self has no comprehension, but my spiritual self, my soul can barely contain itself. The soul knows what is to be. As I let go of this earth, my soul is being born. Minnie, there are no words to explain how I feel. Earthly words would not do justice.'

"Abigail rose from her chair shaking noticeably. She put her hand up on the mantel to steady herself. Turning slightly she appeared to be seeing something I was not.

Moon Dancer

Staring transfixed, she spoke again, saying, 'I tremble at the beauty of it all, while my soul is slowly blotting out my pain. God in His infinite mercy will grant us compassion as we leave this, our earthly home, only to be reborn in heaven.' I listened to her with the tears spilling over and rolling down my cheeks. Once again, she took my hand and said, 'Don't grieve for me. Be happy I am not alone. I am surrounded by those who love me. We are never alone, Minnie. I will pray for you, my dear friend, that you too will one day know the peace that is mine at this moment. This will be my way of continuing our love. We will all be waiting for you. It is all right. I am fine. Just full, I need some time.' She kissed my cheek and said, 'Good night, dear,' then she turned, once again, to the mantel. I left her to her thoughts and silently closed the door. It was the next morning we took her to the hospital."

I am not sure how long Miss Minnie and I and were lost in our own thoughts.

The Room

Miss Minnie smiled as the clock chimed the midnight hour and said, "Well, my dear, you and I just brought in another Christmas. I have to get to bed. We have a long day ahead of us. Most of mine will be at the hospital. Abigail and I have never missed a Christmas since I came here, and the only way I will miss this one is if I go first."

Getting up from my chair, I said "Thank you for telling me about your friend. She truly has had a wonderful life. I can't wait until tomorrow for the rest of her story. I want to know about the fateful day she spoke of." Miss Minnie reached the door, and at my words, she turned with a thoughtful look on her face. Then, with the look of a decision made, she reached for my hand. Taking it, she led me out the door and down the stairs to the next floor. She stopped in front of a large set of rich mahogany doors. She put her hand on the knob, turned, and said to me, "I'm sure Abigail won't mind. I believe she would love for you to see her rooms."

Moon Dancer

We entered, and it was as though I had stepped back in time to a much softer genteel state. My entire being began to slow and fall in step. It was as though I belonged here. Maybe this is why there was no true happiness in my life. It had become too fast; there was no time to just sit and listen. Listening was what I was doing. I could hear the past in the fabric on the walls, the high shuttered windows, the old Queen Anne bed, and a rather large fireplace where a fire softly burned.

Knowing Miss Abigail was not here, I wondered why there was a fire. I turned and asked Miss Minnie, and she replied, "We keep one going in the winter at all times because it takes the chill out of the room. This helps to preserve the portraits and fabrics." I looked around and saw many pictures, but only one dominating the room. It was a very large oval of the most striking couple. It took my breath away. What captivated me was the love, in its purest form. I stood in awe before this beautiful couple, as Miss Minnie spoke with such emotion and love. I had to look at her. She stood straight and proud, with her hands clasped to her chest. She turned and said, "Do you see the love they had—can't you feel it?"

"Yes, it's everywhere in this room," I replied. Miss Minnie smiled and said, "It was their second year anniversary gift to each other. They had a Mr. Samuel Waters from New York commissioned to do the portrait. It was the most extravagant thing they ever did. Abigail had said, 'We want the best, someone who can capture our love, so the many generations to come can always know and feel our love.'" It was obvious that no one would ever have any doubt. It was hanging in the only place to do it justice—over the fireplace. The

The Room

frame of black antique marble was a perfect match to the mantel and hearth that covered almost the entire wall opposite the bed.

Miss Minnie lowered the wall lights to a softer glow, checked the fire and the screen, and said, "Bank the fire when you leave, and please, stay as long as you like. I know she would have wanted you to." I followed her to the door, and as it closed behind her, I found I was alone in another time. Was I intruding? This was *her* life. What business did I have here? Then a feeling of calmness began to spread over me, and I somehow knew she would not mind.

I returned to stand in front of the portrait. I was drawn to it and was once again reminded of how beautifully the artist had captured the very essence of their love. It was as though I was looking at one person and not two, they so mirrored each other. With the fire softly burning and the night sounds of the wind, it was so peaceful. My pain had somehow been eased by the very existence of this lady, her life, and her wonderful Carl. In the stillness, I spoke out loud to them, "I'm so glad you loved her enough to come back and you to wait for him. Miss Minnie did not tell me everything, but somehow you knew he would come back. Where did you find the faith to give your young life to wait?" I smiled when I realized I had been talking to a portrait, as though they were actually here.

Slowly moving about the room, for the first time I realized exactly how many pictures there really were. They were placed in such a manner as not to overwhelm the room. There were pictures of children of all ages—some alone, some in groups with adults, some in school—so many children. "They were all yours," I spoke

Moon Dancer

aloud. It was so natural to talk to her this way.

There was another room, just to the left of the fireplace. I walked in and found it to be what some referred to as a morning room, because it would catch the morning sun. It was an open room with lots of windows covered with soft brocades in yellows, gold, cream, mauve, and dusty pink—very much a lady's room. The essence of the room was a black baby grand piano that dominated the far side of the room by the huge windows. I could picture Miss Abigail sitting, the curtains drawn, allowing full sun and a beautiful view of the hills in the distance. I closed my eyes and let myself drift into the past where soft notes echoed in my mind.

Bringing myself back to the present, I once again continued to become familiar with the morning room. Another fireplace, a small one, which was just the right size for this room, was located behind the larger fireplace of the bedroom. The mantel, hearth, and face were made of small cracked stones. The colors were mixed with beige, soft browns, and ivory. It was most definitely a lady's room.

I found myself wishing I could meet her and get to know this great lady personally. Since she was so ill, I was sure it would be an intrusion. Miss Minnie had planned to spend most of the day with her. I just could not ask. Her time was so close now. I would have to be content with all that I had learned and would learn from Miss Minnie. How wonderful for me to have come to this place at this time. I knew that I was experiencing what Christmas was all about—love and caring for others. The warmth of this place had surrounded me from the moment I had arrived, something I had been missing in my life.

The Room

The feeling of being loved had slowly seeped from me over the period of my illness, which had come about after the death of my husband. Being without him and his love, I had become so alone and empty. Now this place and its history, its love, and its life had spilled over to fill me once again—such magic! Christmas had always been my magic, until the changes. How wonderful it was to feel it again. I said a silent prayer of thanks as I returned to the bedroom.

It was natural for me to walk over and sit on the side of the bed, reach out, and pick up the book lying there. It had a beautiful leatherbound surface of soft pastels, and I opened it without thinking. Realizing what it was, I was both excited and hesitant. Before me were these words: *My Life of Free Will: The Journal of Abigail Hastings.* Wonder and an overwhelming desire began to override my guilt. I could hear the words spoken by Miss Minnie: "Stay as long as you like. I am sure Abigail would not mind." I knew that she would not; this was as it should be.

I started to read, and with each page the life of this truly brave lady began to unfold for me. The answers were all there. Miss Minnie had given me the story of her life. Now Miss Abigail was showing me her life. I found I was living every page with her. I became lost in another time.

The Journal

I have kept other journals over the years. On looking back, I find they are interesting and reminiscent, with the naivete of youth. This is why I rewrite my life with what I pray is wisdom, knowledge, and an insight born of a life well lived. I am praying that I did just that. I thank God for the ability to use His gift of free will—my choices, not others. Others may make demands on me and change the course of my life, but I have the right to use my gift of free will, to choose how to live my life. I have always prayed for God to let me do His will. In doing so, I am completing myself.

Without God we will become lost. How many times have we heard someone say, I have gone as far as I can on my own? I am not sure how I arrived at this stage of my life. My intentions were to never find myself in ruin. We need to understand that we have only simplicity to accomplish. Instead, we become obsessed with what is just out of our sight, searching for what is present in the next day. Then, alas, we are never satisfied, if by chance or a miracle we achieve our goal. Our present is missed because we are longing for a lost past or dreading a part of our future. We seem to never know what to do with our present.

I find now I am only concerned with the future, for much time has passed since I was a child. Now, I am to regress to a place where thinking is not a planned activity, to be free and to do what is not expected of me. In my frail state my mind is the only part of me I cannot see. As it tries to maintain itself, this body is showing signs of a life well lived.

We find that the passage of time allows us a slow steady acceptance of the future, just as one listens to a spring shower while strolling among the flowers. We are getting wet, but the experience of the mind takes away the unpleasantness of the body. Earthly pleasures are often obtained with a sacrifice.

Most would joyfully forfeit all to return to the blessed age of innocence. We search for contentment but are never satisfied. Is it wanting nothing and having nothing, when we truly have it all? Does it lie in death, to come to the end of a lifelong journey? Could it be peace, when all stops and we are released in spirit to be free of earth and body? To be a soul that survives with and in the presence of God? What is the light we hear so much about in a near-death experience? Is revelation what we call consciousness? I believe that my revelation has begun now. I find that the time has come in my life to prepare for death of the body and birth of the soul.

My life's journey has prepared me for this time. I wait with much joy. There will be no sorrow in me because

The Journal

of the promise from God through His Son Jesus Christ, in 1 Corinthians 2:9, "But as it is written, eye hath not seen nor ear heard, neither have entered the heart of man, the things which God hath prepared for them that love him." What a wonderful journey, for this is what life is, a marvelous journey with the gift of free will at the heart of all those wonderful frightening choices.

Now, I will try, with a pen, to put the entirety of my life upon these pages. Why would I, you might ask, try to make a difference, to show that my life did count? What good is knowledge if it is not passed on to be shared by others? How could I have lived more than ninety years and not feel it is worth passing on, all of it, every bitter and sweet moment? When you tally all those moments, they equal life.

Nothing can replace the Bible, the real book of knowledge. It is written in 1 Corinthians 2:5 "that your faith should not stand in the wisdom of many, but in the power of God." The Bible is a journal for the world and mankind, of God and His Son Jesus Christ.

Some would say that birth is the time you begin to live. My body was alive at birth, but I did not really begin to live until Carl came into my life. I already had a good life. I loved my mother and father. They were wonderful parents and people. They loved me and prepared me for my life, which was not to be a copy of theirs. This is when my introduction to free will came about. If I chose to spend the day with my father, to them it was my choice, and they accepted it. My friends and classmates were not allowed to do this.

The farm, lumberyards, and granite quarries were no place for young ladies. My father paid no mind to the opinions of others, much to their dismay. As time passed and his opinion was not swayed, the townspeople grew used to seeing me in places where others were not allowed.

I grew up with a balanced side of life and nature. The birth and death of the livestock slowly introduced me to the loss we sometimes have to face. Time passed, and as I grew older, I was to witness the financial side of running a business. My mother trained me, as well, in the running of the house. Some who worked for Mother and Father, as well as most of the townspeople who came to call, were thought of as equals by me. This was not well liked or agreed upon by most. Such was my life as a child.

My first real trauma was at the age of ten. The stove in the kitchen caused a fire that destroyed most of the house. I had been playing in a room located behind the kitchen. How I loved that place! It was warm and quiet, and I loved the smells. I would play there for hours. In winter, when it snowed, it was my playground. The house was ablaze before I was missed. When they found me, I had been hit by a fallen beam, but somehow I had not been burned. Mother always smiled and would tell me, "That, my child, is because your angel was watching over you." This is also when I started to learn about God and His angels. The more I learned, the more special I began to feel. God had sent one of His angels to watch over me—how wonderful! It had taken several months for me to recover. I had no aftereffects, only the frightening memory, which gradually faded. To this day, if I am in that room, I can still smell the smoke and remember.

The Journal

My father had the house restored and took the opportunity to add other rooms and another floor to the two already there. Over time, it has grown from the small place he and Mother came to when I was a baby.

The kitchen has a most unusual feature. The outside walls and the wall at the back of the room, separating it from the back storage room, were made of stone, which had been acquired from the quarries, as well as the farm. The stone give it such an earthy feel. The long side wall has a large, beautiful fireplace made for cooking as well as warmth. I so enjoyed it there, especially at Christmas. I would sit in front of the old fireplace and make all of my gifts—such fond memories.

☆ ☆ ☾ ☆ ☆

I will now tell you of one of my most joyous days, when I saw Carl for the first time. It was the summer of 1911. I was twelve at the time. Mother and I had gone to town that morning and were preparing to leave for home when he and his father passed by. Carl had a rather somber look to him, but I liked him immediately. I remembered asking my mother who he was and she had answered, "He is Mr. Master Hastings' son, Carl. They have the farm closest to ours on the opposite side of Sutters Pond. Mr. Hastings is a very powerful man, both in spirit and in business. I hear he has great plans for himself and Carl." Later on, I was to learn the truth. Mr. Hastings' family didn't have the power or money to support their son, Carl's father, in a career of politics that he so wanted. When Carl was born, Mr. Hastings saw his chance to achieve his goal through Carl. He compiled a great fortune for that time and became obsessed with using it to educate Carl and launch him into politics. This would enable Mr. Hastings to fulfill his dreams—being by his son's side all the way—making sure he did everything he wanted, ensuring Carl would not fail. This was not what Carl wanted for himself, but Mr. Hastings did not care. He said life would go as planned. Carl was his son and would obey.

I remember telling my mother that I had known of the Hastings, but not about Carl. She said that was because he was always away at school. She believed he was enrolled at the Black Forest Academy, just a few counties to the southeast.

Some would say that fate stepped in a few weeks later, but I like to think God and His wisdom gave me a wonderful gift: the chance to meet my lifelong love and mate while we were still mere children. This is what we were—a child of twelve and a man-child of seventeen. If you had spoken this to us, at that time, we would have been appalled and insulted. It happened at Sutters Pond, which has all my life been my most favorite place. I was allowed the freedom to go where I pleased, as long as I stayed within the limits set by my father. Every free moment I could find, to the pond I went. This was just such a day. I was coming down the path to my spot, which was on a small slope overlooking the pond. You could see our place off in the distance to the right and Carl's to the left. This is why I so loved my spot. We were neighbors, but our farms were not close. Many miles separated us. The closer I came, I could see that someone else was there. In all my time of coming there,

The Journal

I had never seen anyone else. I hesitated and studied him closely, and then I recognized Carl. I slowly approached, and he turned and then stood up. I caught a look of sadness in his eyes, which he quickly covered. I wanted to get rid of the awkward tension between us, so I said, "Hello, my name is Abigail. I live over there," pointing to our place. He said hello and showed me where he lived as well.

We sat down and started to talk. I told him that I came here all the time and that I had never seen him here before. Once again, the sadness touched his face and he replied, "I'm away most of the time at school."

From that day on, we became great friends, and, as time passed, I knew I had grown to love him. Oh, I knew then that I was too young to think in that way, but I also knew I would grow up and become a woman. I knew when I did I would marry Carl. There was no doubt in my mind.

☆ ☆ ☾ ☆ ☆

My father's name was Reginald Charles Duffin and Mother was Eliza Victoria Ashton Duffin—such wonderful names for two very spirited people. Father had compiled a vast fortune since coming to America, to the state of Vermont, when I was only six months old. He had brought a modest sum with him and had taken a few years to become knowledgeable in the business ventures of that time. When he was ready, he began small and worked his way up, becoming immensely successful. He was very secretive about his business ventures and was not a man to hoard his wealth. He taught me to think of others and discreetly share what I had with those less fortunate. One evening he had shared a scripture from the Bible to explain why he helped others. He read 1 Corinthians 13:13, "And now abideth faith, hope, charity, these three; but the greatest of these is charity." I have always tried to remember these words. Because Father never forgot the verse, family and friends in England and America would, from time to time, come into unexplained income, just when they needed it. He neither needed nor wanted notoriety for his generosity. This was the secret of our family.

We lived modestly, relying on the income from the dairy farm and lumber business. We added a few extras in time, but only from profit the farm made. The secret, as it had come to be called by us, was taken care of from a modest office in New York. There was an accountant, an attorney, and a secretary. Though only three, they were the best in their field. My mother and I loved to go to the office. As I stated before, Father did not have the opinions of the time that women were to be sheltered from the matters of men, such as financial matters, politics, and the news of the world. Real estate was where most of the money came from. We were allowed to observe closings of his business dealings. There were three to five of these trips a year. We mostly, however, lived the small-town life.

We shared anonymously in our community, always by surrogates. Yearly donations would appear in the books of churches and organizations. My father relished the chance to do this. How he loved the secret. It never bothered him to care for others of different faiths and

The Journal

religions. He said God saw us as one, and so did he. His only stipulation in regard to how the monies were to be used was to care for the needs of all churches in and around the surrounding community. If there was a need, provide it. This is how, at the age of fourteen, my passion for less fortunate children was born. It was natural for me to develop, from my father, independence to do and think for myself. As a result, helpless children and their independence became my cause to champion.

It was customary for me to walk to and from school, a total of four miles, because most of the children in our area walked. I had asked my father to let me. He was reluctant, but eventually gave in. He knew that I did not want to be treated differently. It was on one of these walks that I witnessed something that would change my life and the lives of many others.

It was early winter, and a light snow had fallen the night before. It was getting cooler and had become dark by midday, a sure sign of more to come. I passed the Walden farm every day. Mrs. Walden has six children, their ages ranging from five to thirteen. Though I knew of them, we were not acquainted. As I grew close to their farm, I remembered that the children had just lost their father last June. Mr. Walden had been killed in a farming accident. The closer I got to the house, I knew something was wrong. The children were crying and shouting. When I grew close enough, I could see Mrs. Walden. She sat on the steps of her porch with her arms wrapped around her waist, rocking back and forth, crying uncontrollably.

Two men and a woman were taking the children away. I recognized one of the men as the minister of the Harmony Methodist Church, close to Quire Town. I had never seen the other man or woman before. They drove away and I just couldn't leave Mrs. Walden alone, but I didn't want to intrude on her grief. Finally, I just went over and sat down beside her. I sat still for some time. She calmed down and slowly turned and looked at me. I placed my hand on her arm and said, "My name is Abigail Hastings. I am sorry, and I do not mean to intrude, but can I help you in any way?" She shook her head and replied, "You are just a child, and you cannot change my life. My husband was killed, and now they have taken my children and my farm. They told me that without my husband here, there is no farm; and no farm leaves me without any means to take care of my children. I have to leave my home in two days." Her eyes were showing emptiness and pain. I had never seen anyone in this state before. It was burned into my memory that day. I have never forgotten.

Mrs. Walden pushed herself up and went toward the door. I asked her once again, as I followed her, "Please, may I help you? Can I get someone for you?"

She turned and said, "Child, only if you can bring back my husband and my babies." This she had said so softly I had to strain to hear her. She placed her hands on the door and looked straight into my eyes and said, "Only if you can give me back my life." I was left alone on the porch, struggling with what I had just seen and heard. I had never been a witness to such despair. I had

The Journal

always been so fortunate. I realized I had yet to experience a situation as painful as this one in my life. I knew the world could be cruel, but I had never been this close to anything like the loss of family and a home. I could not bear it.

    I knew I had to do something. My father would be able to help. He was smart and always had an answer. It was growing darker and getting late. I knew that my parents would be worried. I went to my father and told him all that had happened. He stood with his back to the fire, with a puzzled look on his face and asked, "You said the minister of their church was one of the three people there." I had told him I did not know his name, but I had seen him before and knew who he was. I asked my father why the minister would do this; didn't we give donations to the church? He had answered, "Yes." I asked, "Why then didn't he help her? What happened?" His answer was, "I'm not sure, Abby, but I will find out." With this said, he turned to go. I ran after him, taking his hand. "But, Father, I have to help her. I have to get her children for her. She has to have them tonight. Tomorrow could be too late. You didn't see her. It was her eyes. There was nothing there. Please, Father, I have to go with you. Can't you see this is my place? I have to change this, or I too will forever be changed."

    I did change that day. I grew up. I had left home in the morning a child—yes, older—but still very much a child. Naive about some of the realities of the world, I had returned home later that night a woman, with a maturity I had never known before. My life had afforded me a strong foundation that, over time, would allow me to grow into a well-balanced woman, thanks to my parents.

Moon Dancer

But the experience with Mrs. Walden had caused me to achieve this in one horrible, miraculous day. I had, for the first time in my young life, changed a situation and made a difference in the lives of others.

After going to town, we went to the home of the minister of our church, Mr. Thurston Mauldin. He had ushered us into his study. There, my father had encouraged me to tell of the previous events. When I had finished, Reverend Mauldin reflected for a time by the fire, gazing into the depths as though the answer could be found there.

Slowly, he turned to us. Rubbing his chin, he said, "I'm afraid it may be too late to do anything tonight. First thing in the morning, I will look into the matter." I had bolted from my chair and ran to him, pleading for him not to wait, telling him of the urgency and of the state of Mrs. Walden's mind. I stood waiting as he reconsidered.

Finally he said, "I will see if I can find where they have taken the children and speak to the person in charge." He looked at me and then at my father and said with conviction, "I will have to assure them, meaning the church, and I will take full responsibility for their welfare. The church doesn't have enough in the account to pay for the farm and hire someone to work it for her. It may have already been sold. It was in default. We can, with donations, care for the needs of the family. I am not sure this will be enough to satisfy the authorities, thereby causing them to change their mind." I asked him to please try, and Father asked that our visit be held in strict confidence. We thanked him and left for home. He went to find the children. After talking it through, my

The Journal

father and I decided to discreetly drive to Mrs. Walden's farm and wait. We had to know that night. We would not have been able to sleep otherwise. We waited across the road, hidden in the shadows and growing quite cold. We had used the sleigh and my father's favorite horse. It was a Morgan named Blade. He was such a beautiful horse. I will never forget him. We had been there for about thirty minutes when a car stopped in front of the house; it was the same one that had taken the children away earlier. Mrs. Walden opened the door and stepped out on the porch to embrace her crying, excited children. From the shadows that night, I had witnessed the consuming love of a mother for her children and the importance of family. Seeing the children as they were taken away and now being returned, I could see why God had made mothers. These children looked to her for their existence. They were lost without her, and without them she would lose her sense of being. On the ride home that night I looked at my father and, for the first time, thought of a life without him and Mother. I shuddered at the overwhelming emptiness I felt, praying that this would never happen and thanking God for them.

Over the next few days we found out just what had happened to the Waldens. My father had gotten word to his New York office, and they had hired a Mr. Frank Wheeler, a private detective. He would find out what had happened to this family and why their church had not used the donated funds to help them. This explanation would be another life-alerting lesson for me.

Mr. Wheeler conducted all of his business with only the New York office. This he did to keep our family totally out of the matter. When he had finished his

49

investigation, he sent his report to New York, and they sent it on to us. After dinner, on the evening of the arrival of the report, my father had asked my mother and me to sit with him in the library, his favorite room. Then revealed the information in the report.

Mr. Wheeler had first looked into the background of the minister, a Mr. Jack Blanchard, and the church accounts. There were no funds in the account, only enough to keep the doors open. The money that had been donated each year by my family, as well as the church members, had never been credited to the account. Large amounts had been deposited in a separate account opened by the minister. He came to serve Harmony Methodist Church five years earlier. From the very beginning, he only kept enough money in the church's account to run the church. On three other occasions, over the five-year period, three fathers from the congregation died, leaving widows with small children. In each case the widow lost her farm, and her children were taken and eventually adopted. Mr. Wheeler found that the farms had the notes paid off by Minister Blanchard. He claimed he was buying them for the church to give back to the families who had lost them.

But, in fact, they were sold to some of the more wealthy and powerful men in the area. These men looked down on the less fortunate of their fellow men. They were men without hearts and were greedy for power. After the sale of each farm, the money was deposited into the account of Minister Blanchard. Along with the charitable donations from my father and the church members, he was making quite a fortune for himself.

Mr. Wheeler was making plans to leave for New York.

The Journal

He was content with his findings and his report, but could not shake the feeling that there was still something missing. That same evening, this feeling was to come back to him as he was having dinner. He overheard two men at the next table, talking about Mrs. Walden and her children. They were discussing how there had been an anonymous donation that had saved her farm and her children from being adopted and how it was a shame that Oscar had been killed. He was a hard-working man, and they had never known him to take chances. One of the men said, "No man in his right mind would have hooked up a load of feed in that manner. That was just asking for trouble." The other man commented, "There is not a farmer around here who would have done that. He would surely have been killed just as Oscar was."

The word *killed* was what bothered Wheeler. What if Oscar had been killed and it was made to look like a farm accident. Then he knew what was bothering him, the question he had not been able to put into words. What were the chances of four men in the past five years all dying in the same manner, and all belonging to the same church? Furthermore, these were men who were experienced at farming. These men knew the dangers involved and would not have taken the kinds of chances that they supposedly took. It was too much of a coincidence. He went back to the boarding house, told the clerk he was staying, sent off a letter to New York, and set out to find who had killed these men.

One week later, Mr. Wheeler found that Minister Blanchard had hired a man from his hometown, one of his childhood friends. His name was Paul Shank. He just came in and staged the deaths to look like farm-related accidents and left. Clean. The deaths here made Mr. Wheeler curious about the minister's past. He checked his background and found that two men from the minister's previous congregation were killed in farm-related accidents, along with one man from the congregation before that. Apparently, the minister had grown more greedy, bold, and confident over the years. He presumed he would get away with it again, as he always did. Mr. Wheeler had written in his detailed report to father, "I am proud to report Paul Shank and Jack Blanchard are both behind bars and awaiting a court trial. There is no way they will be let go. There is too much evidence."

My father looked at my mother and then walked over to me and said, "If it had not been for the compassion of a young lady walking home from school, seeing someone in need, and having the courage to get involved—determined to make a difference—we would not have uncovered any of this. He would have continued to do these bad things, ruining the lives of so many people. Your mother and I are so very proud of you. Thank you for being such a wonderful daughter."

I had never realized that there were such cruel people in the world. It was a shock to me, yet I was determined to remain focused on the beauty that was also present in the world. The report and Mr. Wheeler's summary were still on my mind as I tried to sleep. When I went down for breakfast, I asked my father if we could try to find the children of the other families and bring them together again. I wanted to give them money to get started. He said we could. He would have to get with Mr. Wheeler that morning to secure his services. Father was sure he was still in town, but due to leave that morning.

The Journal

Later, we were informed that the three earlier families could not be reunited. Most of the children were grown and the files sealed. Mr. Wheeler could not find out who had adopted them. But the other three that were in our community had their families restored. Money had been placed in bank accounts for each of them. No one had any idea who had donated the money or how the minister was exposed.

When Mrs. Walden was asked if she knew how she got her children back, just hours after they were taken, she replied that she did not know. All she could remember, because she had been so upset, was a young girl who had asked, "What can I do? Is there anything I can do for you?" She said she remembered looking at this young girl, and saying, "What can you possibly do? My whole life is gone, I have lost everything." When the girl asked, "What can I do for you?" Mrs. Walden said she felt crazy and remembered saying, "You can give me back my family. Can you do that?" Mrs. Walden recalled: "I slammed the door in her face and fell on the floor crying. Two hours later my children were returned to me. What if this young girl was an angel and I slammed the door in her face?" She looked up in wonder, her arms around her children and said, "You know, I do believe she was an angel." It has always made me smile that she thought of me as an angel, but I knew it would take a lifetime of hard work to achieve that goal.

Carl and I had said nothing to anyone about our meeting at the pond. I did not tell my parents, even though we had always had a good relationship. This was too new. I was dealing with feelings I could not explain. I wanted my parents to think of me as smart and in control. When

53

Moon Dancer

it came to Carl and my feelings, I was unsure of what to say, so I did not say anything. Since we only saw each other when he was home from school, a few times a year, no one would notice.

It was Christmas, and Carl would be home for the holidays. I was so excited because Christmas was my most favorite time of the year. How I enjoyed the Christmas tree, the presents, the food—and I loved to cook. We always decorated the house with lots of beautiful things. The snow—how it really turned our place into a wonderland.

I could not wait to go to the pond. It was always frozen by this time of year and so beautiful, with the snow on the ground. We were to meet after lunch on Christmas Eve. My happiness was so apparent. I just could not hide it. Everyone thought it was the holiday. I had no idea how my life was about to change. I bundled myself up, and off I went to see Carl. I was so excited to give him the present I had made; it was hidden in my cloak.

When I arrived at the pond, Carl was not there. I was content with the beauty all around me. A light snow had started to fall. The sky did not look heavy, so I was not concerned about being caught in a storm. I knew if I were caught in a snowstorm, however, it would be easy to become disoriented and freeze only minutes from safety. The pond was solid ice and sent back twinkling lights as the sun played upon it. The fir trees were all heavy with snow. Only a few birds and small animals scurried about. I heard the horse approaching. I ran to the clearing, expecting Carl to be in his usual light-hearted mood, only to find him somber with a hard look upon his face. He just sat upon his horse and

The Journal

stared at me, not saying a word. He had grown into a man; somehow I had not noticed. When we laughed and sat side-by-side talking away the time, I had not seen it. Now, upon his horse, in his rigid pose, there looking at me was a man.

For the first time since we met, I felt like a child. I was apart from him, more distant than the few feet that separated us. Finally, he dismounted, walked over, put his arms around me without saying anything. We stood quietly for some time. Then, he put his hands on my arms and held me away from him and said, "Abby, I must go. I cannot stay." I said, "But, you can't go; you just got here, and I have your present." I went to reach for it, almost in tears. Then he said, "No, you do not understand. I have to leave my father's house. I have to leave school." Then he hesitated, with tears in his eyes, he said, "I have to leave you, too. I don't know where I am going, but I cannot take my father any more."

My mind was reeling as he talked, and I tried to keep up with all that he was saying. "My father just informed me that he has made arrangements with Mr. Fred Willard, over in Chittenden County, for me to marry his daughter at the end of my school term. After the marriage, my new father-in-law, Mr. Willard, is to set me up in prominent circles and bring me into his firm, grooming me for political office. We are to live with her parents." I stood in disbelief at what I heard. All I could say was, "Carl, you cannot marry her, and you cannot leave me." "I have to go. If I stay, he will make me miserable for the rest of my life. Abby, I am afraid I will hurt him one day. I cannot take it anymore. I'm sorry. I have to go." With this, he got back on his horse and rode away.

Moon Dancer

The next morning, I went back to our place. I found the letter. I have placed it now between these pages.

Abby,

I cannot stay here with you. I can't. I feel like I am suffocating. Even the barns and the stench—funny, I never seemed to notice before. I find the things I have grown accustomed to now seem to be pressing in on me. I feel I can't breathe. Abby, I love you, but even you are stifling me. Everyone wants me to be, to do, to stay, and to conform. Everything has always been set for me, preplanned. Not one person ever asked me what I wanted for my life. No one cared how I would feel.

Standing here on this hill, looking out over the land with its openness and beauty, I still feel trapped. The fact that it will be mine someday is still a burden. I am so sorry these things are of no interest to me. I do not want it, and I do not want a life with you, not now. It is too much. I am being crushed with the weight of it all.

Can't you see? I have to go. I have to see what is out there, experience all that I can before the time comes when I am no longer here. I know I am not being fair, or very nice. I have a lot of nerve asking you this, Abby. Will you wait for me? At least, as long as you can. You were raised to be a wife and mother. Family is very important to you. At this time, I am frightened to death of these things. You frighten me most of all, for if I stay and we marry,

The Journal

you will grow to despise me, for I feel I will become a bitter old man who let the world pass him by. I cannot stand leaving you, but more than that, I cannot stand the thought of you hating me. So, I will add coward to my many wrongs.

I cannot face you, so I sit in our favorite place and take the easy way out. I write to you of how I feel, hoping you will understand. Please don't hate me too much. Stay strong. Try to keep loving me, even though I don't deserve your love. Always remember that I leave because of me, not you.

I know not where I go, so I cannot tell you. I know not what to say, so I will not write. I know not when I will return, so I will not promise. I only know I truly do love you and how unfair this is to you.

When you wake and read this, I will be gone. I write to you and Mother only. I cannot face anyone. Please, speak for me. I know I have no right to ask. Tell them what you wish or tell them nothing at all. I am past caring. I hope someday you will be able to forgive me.

Carl

☆ ☆ ☾ ☆ ☆

I went through each following day in shock and disbelief. I waited for a letter that never arrived. As time slowly passed, I put Carl in a special place in my mind and heart. I became interested in life around me again and spent more time with my father. He once made a remark to

Moon Dancer

me about my absence. "Well, it is nice to have you back again, little lady. I thought you had outgrown your dad." I laughed and said, "I guess I was trying to grow up." In my heart, I had found a peace. I had prayed and asked God to watch over Carl, to send His angels to guide him and someday bring him home to me.

I had no desire to see other boys. I politely turned down any offers, only accepting invitations in groups and numbers of more than two. I was friendly, but detached. In time, the young men stopped asking. We were just friends, all of us, friends. As the years passed, I became involved in school. I worked on the school newspaper, and I volunteered to tutor other students who were having learning problems.

We still went to New York each year, where I became more involved in the business. On one of my visits, my father had arranged for me to be taught about the buying and selling of property and land. I had an aptitude for figures and was quick to learn. Each time I went I would learn something new. Once, on a visit, I met my father's lawyer, Mr. Abrams Sr. He and Father were discussing a colleague who had made a bad investment and had gotten in trouble with the law. I became fascinated with all he was saying and found, for the first time, a real passion for learning, especially about law. All the different laws intrigued me. Some laws, to me, were sound and reasonable, while others made no sense. Some just made me mad. When I asked, "How can you get rid of the bad laws?" Mr. Abrams had answered, "You have to understand the law in order to change it." I knew that day that this was what I wanted to do. I asked, "Can women be lawyers?" My father laughed and said, "I don't know about other women, but you have never let the fact of being a woman stop you from doing anything you set your mind to." So, I walked out of the office that day with a direction in mind for my life.

By day I went to school and helped my father. At night I studied law, every aspect of it. Father's library slowly began to grow. My knowledge grew right along with it. To me, the arrival of each new book was far from satisfying. It only opened a need for another one.

My father jokingly remarked to Mother one night at the dinner table, as he smiled and winked at me, "Our little girl seems to possess a need for books as much as Mr. Willis' prize porker devours all the slop he can find and just keeps looking for more." My mother had laughed as she feigned indignation and replied, "Please, Father, just look at our beautiful little Abby. She in no way puts me in mind of a fat, ugly swine." As we laughed, I thought how wonderful to have them. I loved them so much, and our lives were beautiful.

In time, when I became a woman and a wife, I found my mind recapturing many of those golden moments. They nourish us and give us inner peace and place a smile upon our face. With a proper, loving childhood, our lives as adults are more attainable. For all the negatives (and there will be those) we have the positives from our foundation. I found I would need these days, need the knowledge, and draw on the love I stored and packed tightly in my memory. I found a strength I never knew I possessed. One I found, with the passage of time, was the mirror image of my parents. Strange how, as a child, you do not notice all the really important aspects of life. When you begin to mature, suddenly they are there. Those early years are all that matter in life, but I am starting to get ahead of myself again.

    I have to bring in, now, another wonderful chapter in my life. That was the day Miss Minerva Lee Perkins walked through our door and into our hearts. She became an employee of our house, but most important of all, she became a lifelong friend. Just a few hours ago, before I took up my pen to write, she and I shared yet another evening by the fire that we so enjoy: tea and the reminiscing of two elderly ladies who can remember the polished stairs, twinkling lights, and the smells and sounds of a warm and loving home. Crisp summer dresses, colored ribbon in one's hair, the smell of spring, the soft summer rain, and all the more important things in life. When they were yours and were happening, somehow they had no importance at all and only became so when they were lost to you. How very dear, to share with a true and devoted friend. When I looked at my Minerva—as I choose to call her now, for she is all that I have left in this world—I do not see a small elderly lady whose hair is as white as snow, piled softly around an equally small head, as she absently smooths back a stray piece of hair. I do not see an aged hand with the skin of time. A hand placed softly on a cheek that has lost the color and the touch of youth. I can still see her standing by the fire as she waited for Mother, Father, and me to enter the room. Holding out her delicate hand she smiled her beautiful smile, which she has shared with me for these many, many years.

    After we had each introduced ourselves, she handed my mother (not my father) a paper of reference. She stood quietly as my mother read the contents and passed

The Journal

it to Father. I remember how young and pretty she was, and how proud. Strange, how someone can look proud: not smug, or conceited, just proud. My father spoke, "You are quite young, Miss Perkins, for a position as head of the house. But, I must say, for a woman of your years, you certainly have acquired your knowledge and served your time well. Father turned, and looking at Mother, he said, "Don't you think so, Mother?" I had just finished reading, as well. He also looked at me and asked, "And you, Abigail?" Both Mother and I agreed with my father.

Still looking at us he said, "In that case, do both of you agree with me that we should welcome Miss Perkins to our home?" We both stood smiling and said, "Yes." My father turned to shake her hand, saying, "We would be most delighted to have you accept this position in our home. Furthermore, this will be your home, and we want you to think of it as such. Run it as you would yours, and we will all be happy."

Even to this day, from time to time, she will protest when I attempt to do anything for her. In the early days her constant comment was, "I am in charge of this house, and it is my place to care for you and not you to care for me." How my father loved to tease her. He remarked many times that he loved to tease her. I really believe they both enjoyed the back and forth altercations.

One of my favorite stories is how Minnie got her call name. We were all at dinner one evening. My father had once again coerced Minerva to dine at our table. Father had asked, "With your name being Minerva, how did you come to be called Minnie?" She had been a little abashed to be the center of conversation. Looking at each of us, she put down her fork and looked straight at my father. She said, "If you promise not to laugh, I will tell you." We each promised, and Father threw a sideways wink at me, which she saw. Considering this, she said to him, "You promised." He had put on a very sincere look and said very strongly, "I promise." My mother and I both laughed, and Minnie continued. "My mother would tell me the story many times. She and I so enjoyed it. On one of the rare occasions, she had gone to town. When passing a store window, there was a very small porcelain doll, the first one she had ever seen. She was curious but a little embarrassed to go in, for she felt the owner would know she could never afford such an item. Gathering her courage, she went in and asked about the doll. To her surprise, the shopkeeper was very kind.

"He informed her it was called a miniature, since it was small and exquisite. On the day I was born, she remembered the doll. Thinking how like the miniature I was, and that my given name was too great for my size, she chose to call me Minnie. Telling me, she recognized in time I would grow to my name."

Father, true to his promise, smiled and said, "I have to agree with your mother. Minerva Lee is still too large for a little one like you." Father smiled and asked, "Would you care for more tea?" This is how our life was.

☆ ☆ ☾ ☆ ☆

About a year later, life was to alter once again. I was to learn more about the wonderful and very frightening gift of free will. When we are at the time of decision

The Journal

and are alone, we can become bewildered not knowing the end result.

It was the first day of April, such a beautiful day. A soft breeze was blowing. The flowers and trees were swaying. My father and I enjoyed the walk together on our way to the dairy barns. Everyone would be busy, for it was milking time. The milk had to be taken to the creamery where it was processed for shipment. The creamery and train depot were only a few hundred feet apart. This was to ensure faster loading. The train had a milk car, which was refrigerated with ice. In order for the milk to reach the consumer within twenty-four hours from milking time, the milk car had to meet a milk train on the main line. This procedure is different from the way milk is processed today. Back then, they would only strain the milk, cool it down, and pour it into a sterilized container for shipment.

When we reached the barns there was much activity, everyone to their own chore. How I loved the farm, the smell of the hay, and the newborn calves. I loved to watch them frolic about. Father had gone over to speak to one of the men. When they finished, he called to me. I ran up to him; wrapping his arm around my shoulder, he said, "Since this is going to be my last trip to New York before your eighteenth birthday, what would you like for your mother and me to pick out for you? Or would you prefer a surprise?" I had smiled up at him and said, "A surprise. You know how I love your and Mother's surprises." He had said, "Then, a surprise it will be. We wish you could accompany us, dear. We understand that you have your studies and exams to take. How does it feel to be on the threshold of a new life as a grown woman?"

Moon Dancer

My answer had been, "Very exciting and a little intimidating." He had smiled and said to me with one of his winks, "You will do just fine. After all, you come from good stock." Father had used this as one of our jokes and as part of the playfulness of his character. But, I would remember this remark many times in the years to come. What was expressed as a joke has, in fact, been the very thing that has kept me moving, pressuring me to achieve my goals. I was made of good stock. They were the best parents one could hope to have.

Weather permitting, we would have a light lunch on the side porch. We enjoyed the shade from our beautiful tree. After lunch we went in to prepare for Mother and Father's departure to the city. All was a flurry of activity. Minnie had seen to the packing and had the cases placed in the carriage. Father loved to travel about the community in this manner rather than in the automobile. He had purchased one just the year before and used it only for longer trips.

I had been waiting for them at the foot of our beautiful staircase. I have always loved those stairs. I'm not sure exactly why. Maybe because of the way Father had always come bounding down them, as he was doing then. He took two or three steps at a time. I always marveled that he never once stumbled. Reaching the bottom, he came up to me, adjusting his tie and cuff links. He turned for me to examine him and give my approval, which I always did. He was a handsome man: about five feet eleven inches tall, a medium complexion, soft sandy blond hair, and those twinkling blue eyes. He was well built from farm work, but not overly so.

With my nod of approval, he had given a small bow

The Journal

and asked, "Would you be so kind as to dance with me, young lady, whilst we wait upon that woman you call Mother?" I started to giggle uncontrollably; then he swept me up in his arms, as he had done so many times before. There was never music, only his singing. We waltzed around the room in sheer bliss.

There was a tapping sound and a clearing of my mother's throat. We looked up. She was standing there at the top of the stairs. She was so beautiful. Throwing her head back, she looked at Father with her hands on her hips and said, "Well, is this how you carry on behind my back? Do you have no shame?" When we both started to laugh, she pretended to be hurt. In a very haughty voice, she said, "I think I may just change my mind after all and not go with you, Mr. Reginald Duffin." She began to laugh and run, for my father had taken the stairs in three leaps, and grabbing hold of her, he said, "You just try woman, you just try." With this they kissed. I had always found their show of affection so beautiful and was never embarrassed by it. It was wonderful to know they had such love for each other.

Looking back, it appears that every moment of that day was to be special. So many memories I would cherish forever. My last memory of that day was one of Minnie and me as we stood on the porch waving them off with our heartfelt good-bye. They waved and called to us, saying, "Take care of each other. We will see you at the end of the week." We had followed, waving until they vanished from sight.

That was the last time I was to see my parents alive. I do not know how I managed the days and endured the months to come. If it had not been for my faith in

Moon Dancer

God and His wisdom for our lives, I know I would not have been capable of accepting my fate. Then, there was Minnie. She was in shock, as well. But she held me up when I was down; she always gave me a push. She never left me. She gave me space when needed, but was never far away. I have often thought that God sent Minnie to us. He knew I would need her. I could not be alone after my parents' death. I have never failed to thank Him each and every day for sending her to us.

I will now tell you how this all came to pass. I remind you now that whenever they were on one of their trips, those who knew us just thought they were on a holiday. With my birthday and graduation coming up, this was thought of as well. I am afraid I may be starting to wander again. The mind tends to as we advance in age. I choose to think of it as so much stored knowledge from a very full life. It starts to spill over once a small portal is allowed to open.

☆ ☆ ☾ ☆ ☆

Minnie and I went on with the day-to-day matters of our lives. She managed the house so smoothly. She never once failed at anything; if she did, I was never made aware of it. Many times I had asked myself, "If I were in charge of the house, could I do it at such a young age?" For most women in that position, they were at the other end of their life instead of the beginning.

I went about my day as usual, starting at sunrise in pants, shirt, and boots, with my hair piled under a floppy hat. I made rounds on the farm with Father's overseer,

The Journal

Wade Thompson. He and his family lived nearby. Wade had been with my father since the very beginning. He had watched me grow and always played with me as a child. He now gave me the respect he would give my father; not many men would, with me being a woman. But, Father's ideas about women and business had, over the years, come to make sense to Mr. Wade and others on the farm. But there would always be those who would have a one-sided view.

As we attended to the farm and made plans for the rest of the week, I smiled to myself and thought of the real reason for my parents' trip. The trip was about Mr. Wade and his family. His son Drew was to graduate from high school in June. He so wanted to go to agricultural college in Burlington, but this was not possible. Father paid Mr. Wade well, but he had ten children to feed and clothe. Once, in a conversation, Mr. Wade had absently remarked and then became immediately embarrassed, "I have ten children, and how is it you only have one?" Father laughed heartily and patted him on the back, saying, "You are just a better man than I, Wade." At this, Mr. Wade also laughed, and the tension passed.

Neither of them knew I was in the other stall, cleaning it out. At first, I giggled to myself, and then what he said came clear to me. I had never given it a thought as to why I was the only child. Everyone in this area had average size to large families.

But I am straying again. Mr. Wade could not afford to send his son Drew to college and had asked my father if Father could take him on full time at the farm. Father said to him, "I do not need another full-time man here, Wade, but I would be glad for Drew to split his time between here and the lumber business." Mr. Wade's face had dropped a little, but when my father mentioned the lumber business, he was so happy. He just could not wait to tell Drew.

When Father turned from Wade, he was the one who was wearing the biggest grin, for this was the reason for the trip to New York. Mother and Father had followed Drew's progress all through school. They knew him to be very smart and at the top of his class. He was a hard worker, both on the farm and at school. My parents decided to reward his hard work with an anonymous scholarship to the college of his choice, which was the Agricultural College in Burlington. Father had said, "They are hard-working people, fair and honest. What I admire most about Wade is that he has never once thought of, and never will think of, asking us for help. This is the reasoning behind my decision."

No one, apart from me, would ever know the real reason for my parents' trip. One can say, "Oh, only if they had not gone. If there had not been that reason, they would still be here." Would they, after all? Is there a time for us to be born and a time for us to die? As in the quote from the Bible, James 4:14, "Whereas ye know not what shall be on the morrow. For what is your life? It is even a vapour, that appeareth for a little time, and then vanisheth away."

After seeing to the farm and making plans for the next day, I dressed for school and attended my classes. I had exams all that week. In the evening, Minnie and I had dinner together, and, as she did with my father, she fought me on the idea. Her answer was, "No one else dines with the family; it is not my place." I would answer,

The Journal

"It is your place. I ask you, and you are family." Well, she still to this day argues with me.

All was made ready for my parents' return. I asked for a festive feel to the evening, a meal that was a little different, served with wine. I could not convey the real reason for the celebration. They thought of me as happy to have them home. When the time came and went for their return, I became anxious, as did Minnie. She tried to hide her uneasiness, but mine was there for all to see. As the night began to fall, I knew something was wrong.

Minnie and I were in the sitting room when we heard the knock on the door. Minnie went to answer, for we knew it was not my parents. They would not have knocked. I stayed where I was, in my chair. I felt frozen; even if I had tried, I do not think I could have moved. A fear so powerful had descended over me. It seemed that I held my breath the entire time it took for Minnie to answer the door and escort Mr. Savage into the room. Mr. Walter Savage was the constable in our area. When he approached, all I could see were his boots. I could not look at his face. I just could not. He stood for a moment, wringing his hat. I wanted to bolt and run, but I could not move.

There was another pair of boots behind his. How strange, I thought; all these years I had seen Walter, and I had never looked at his boots before. How strange to only see a man from his waist up. "Miss Abigail," he beseeched. I wanted to cover my ears, not listen. I just could not listen. "Miss Abigail, child, please listen to me." He came down on his knees, took me by the arms. "Child, I am so sorry, but there were heavy rains outside of New York and no one knew. Part of the railroad tracks had been washed away, causing the train to derail." He hesitated, "I am so sorry, child, there were no survivors." My beautiful parents, they were gone. They lay somewhere cold, wet, and alone. They had never been alone. They had never been cold. "Where are they?" was spoken. I think it was I. I am not sure. His answer was, "They have been taken to…" he hesitated again, "Mr. Skinner's place." I knew he was avoiding saying the undertaker. I could not say it either. "When can I go to them?" "Child, don't go tonight. You let us take care of them for you." I said, more firmly, "I have to go to them." He hesitated a moment and said, "In the morning, child, in the morning." Knowing that he was right, I raised my head for the first time and looked at him, straight in the eyes. My mother and father were always by each other's side. When he left home, she went with him. They were always together. "Tell Mr. Skinner to put them together; do not separate them." He began to speak, with an intake of breath, shaking his head, "But, child, this is just not done." "Why not?" I asked, "What will it hurt? Whose business is it anyway? Tell him to put them together." I did not move my eyes till I had finished. I once more focused on his boots. As he once again stood up, he asked, "Is there anything else I can do for you?" I answered, "Tell Mr. Skinner I will see him in the morning." With this, he turned and walked away. The other boots followed. To this day, I do not know who was in those boots. I could hear him talking to Minnie, but I could not understand what was being said.

Minnie helped me up, and together we went up to my room. There we held on to each other and wept for our loss: me, for the wonderful parents of mine, my friends,

The Journal

my loves, the stabbing force of my young life, the loss of their laughter, their smiles, the joy of seeing them kiss, the sheer essence of their presence. Minnie wept for me as well as for her loss. She loved them as I loved them. She had just not loved them as long. Her memories were shorter than mine, but her pain was as deep.

We woke with bright sunlight filling the room and the sounds of life going on as usual. We had fallen asleep upon my bed, still dressed from the day before. I thought, *How can the world have the audacity to continue?* I had not realized I had spoken aloud. Minnie said, as she came to my side, "They would will the world to exist, if only for the reason that you are still in it." I placed my arms around her and said, "Thank you; you always know just what to say."

When Minnie and I arrived at the funeral parlor, Mr. Skinner was waiting for us. He took my hand and gave me his sympathy. I asked, "Why have you not consoled Miss Minnie? She too has lost loved ones." He quickly apologized and spoke to Minnie. I asked to see my parents, and he said he needed to speak with me for a moment before we went in. He said, "It's about your wish, Miss Abigail. This is most irregular. This is not the proper way." "Why, Mr. Skinner?" I had asked, "Who decides these things? I thought the family of the deceased were the ones who made the decisions." "Well, yes, they are Miss Abigail," he replied, "but this is just not normal." "Why, Mr. Skinner? Just because no one before me has asked does not mean it is wrong. After all, someone has to be first. This is my decision. Did you do what I asked?" "Yes," he answered, "they are together." He led the way into the darkened, somber room. There were

71

candles partially circling the casket. This was the only thing I had liked about the room. It, in some small way, had put back a bit of warmth that had been taken. As Minnie and I stood before the casket, Mr. Skinner began backing from the room, saying, "If you should need me, I will be just outside."

    As Minnie and I held on to each other, the light played softly upon the faces of my beautiful mother and father. I smiled and looked at Minnie, saying, "I did right, didn't I? I did right." Minnie looked back at their faces and softly said, "Yes, Miss Abby, you did right. They look like they are smiling," and they did. I felt a sense of peace come over me. Their death would never be right, but my life somehow would be right someday. I also knew that they went the only way they could have, and that was together. Lying here in sleep, in each other's arms, never to be alone. "Go together in love, to God. Wait for me, for I will see you again. Thank you both for my life and for your love. You are my joy and will reside in my heart for as long as it will beat." I spoke the Lord's Prayer, and Minnie joined me as we both said, "Amen." It seemed that all of the candles flickered in union. She and I looked at each other, and Minnie whispered, "I think they heard us and that was their way of letting us know." I had said, "I would like to think so." Taking Mother's hand, I slowly removed the small gold band. Then taking the matching band from Father's hand, I clutched both bands tightly. Whispering softly, I said, "I will always cherish these symbols of your love. I will miss you. God bless you." Minnie said her good-byes and followed me out of the room. When we entered the outer room, Mr. Skinner was waiting. He asked if everything was to my request.

The Journal

I answered, "Yes, thank you. Please, close the casket and do not open it again. Announce there will be a graveside service only, and all who wish to attend may do so.

"Mr. Skinner," I asked, "would you see to the arrangements for me and tell Reverend Mauldin that I can receive him at eleven this morning?" Feeling that I had, in my grief, been rude to him, I touched his hand and said, "I am sorry if I have offended you. I know you do not approve of my arrangements. Thank you so much for conceding to my wishes. My parents look so beautiful together." With this said, his face relaxed, and he pressed my hand as well and said, "You are happy. That is all that matters. I will take care of everything. God bless you, child."

I do not remember the ride home or much of the rest of the day. I was numb. There was just enough lucidity for me to cope. This was a blessing and was needed when I received Reverend Mauldin. After showing him to the sitting room, Minnie excused herself and went to prepare tea. I could see that he too was very distraught. He and my parents were very close. We consoled each other and spent the better part of an hour making preparations for the service. There was to be a graveside service at 10:00 a.m. Reverend Mauldin would deliver the eulogy. Elam Maddox, a deacon of our church and close friend of Father and Mother's, would then do a tribute. Bertha, his daughter, would close the service with my father's favorite song "I Will Meet You in the Morning." Minnie had served tea with my favorite cakes. I sipped the tea that had no taste and could not eat a cake for fear I should choke. Minnie remained close but very discreet.

I awoke early the next morning to a sound I had never

73

heard before, but I knew immediately what it was. Men were preparing a place for my parents under their tree. I will never forget the sound and what it represented; in time I have come to accept the deaths of my parents. What a wonderful mind God has given us with its ability to survive. All we have to do is listen to its dictates, which, when allowed to be governed by the soul, will ultimately guide us in times of sorrow to a healing place and to success in other facets of our life.

My parents had brought the tree, which was an English oak, all the way from England, the Isle of Man, where they had lived in their first home together as man and wife. They often shared their story with me. Every time, they had made it new. They had protected and nurtured the little tree. Mother and Father's story of the trip over was always with them giggling uncontrollably as Father narrated. He would hold the little tree close to him under his cloak as he and Mother, who was holding me, strolled down the deck of the ship. When there was no one to observe them, he would hold his cloak open so the little plant could take in the sun. He tried so hard not to laugh, as he said, "They would think me daft, such a big man, holding me little tree in the sun." We would collapse with laughter.

There was no other place for them to be other than under their little tree. Now it was a big tree and could return the favor. It could shelter and care for them. For all my misery, there was a smile at that thought. I had begun to realize then, as I now know, the good or bad we do can somehow, on occasion, come back to us. This time it was very special. We have, since then, referred to it as Little Tree.

The Journal

We gathered the next day under Little Tree for the service. I was overwhelmed at the large number of people who were there. I began to feel a panic coming over me. Minnie had noticed, for she squeezed my hand and gave me her warm smile. She was my stabilizer. The service was beautiful. I have appreciated it more in the last few years. The longer I am away from that day, the more I remember. So many to hug, shake our hands, and give their condolences.

Minnie and I had said our good-byes and thanked everyone. When we reached the porch, a strange man approached. There was with him a young woman in her early twenties. She was walking in the gardens and paying no attention to us. He shook my hand and, indicating the woman, said, "My name is Fred Willard, and she is my daughter, Christina Emerald. We live in Montpelier. We had to come by to pay our respects when we heard of your loss. We will leave you now, but will call on you this Sunday in the afternoon." He had not waited for an answer, just smiled and hurried away. He called Christina, who did not seem to be in any hurry. She was walking very slowly and looking around. She had been to the side of the house where the dairy barns were located and on her way back had come by way of the porch, looking in the windows as she passed. Saying her good-byes, she had joined her father, and they left in one of the finest of new automobiles. We watched them drive away, and Minnie looked at me and remarked, "I have a very bad feeling. This visit was not a good one, and that lady has something on her mind. She is bad news. They did not come here to see you. They came to look." We both had the same feeling,

75

but we had to let the future take care of itself, because we had the present to see to.

When we entered the foyer, I turned to Minnie and asked, "How shall I live without them?" Her answer will forever be with me and has sustained me these years past. "You will rise every day as you have so many times before, only you will change one thing. Look inside for them. Their smiles and laughter you will see and hear. When you need an answer, listen intently. You know their wisdom. It will never fade. You have to keep them alive, Abby." Touching my heart she said, "Keep them alive here."

I lay in bed the next morning, looking up at the ceiling, not sure if I wanted to cry, scream, or die. Minnie's words came back to me. "You will rise each day as you have so many times before." So I did just that, no more thinking. I jumped up, put on my work clothes, and went to see to the farm. The more I did, the more I wanted to do. I found I could take out my anger on the hay. I jabbed my pitchfork hard and threw it. Then I rolled bales of it around all over the barn. I cleaned out stalls. When I had finished my work, I ran all the way to Sutters Pond. There I fell down on Carl's and my favorite spot. I cried as I had never cried before, till there was nothing left, just a spent young girl who, but for Minnie, was for the first time totally alone. There were no relatives now, none here in America, only very distant cousins in England, whom I would never see. I had lost Carl and now my parents. I could not stop shaking. I let the sun warm and soothe me. I watched as it played about on the water. As always, I could feel the nearness of God. Here was my sanctuary, my church.

The Journal

The tranquility of this place eased me. I could hear in the silence God speaking to my soul, telling me, "Be still, My child. I will never leave you. I will always be here, and when it is your time, I will bring you home." When the feeling of such a tremendous loss started to come over me, I closed my eyes. Now with the calmness circulating within me, I opened them. I let my place envelop me. I stopped shaking. I did not feel alone anymore. I lay on my back and let the peace restore me. When I woke, the sun was on the distant side of the pond. I knew it was well after noontime. That day would bring about an emotional change in my life.

I began walking the fields and pastures at night. The night wind, blowing about my body, was soothing to me. My hair was long and dark, like my mother's. It reached to my waist. I let it hang loose so the wind could blow it about with my long flowing dress. It would move them both about effortlessly. I always found myself drawn to the same place, standing on the knoll overlooking the pond, with the beautiful night all around me. No matter what the night brought, to me it was always flawless.

Unlike my parents, I had dark eyes. My father called them hunting cats' eyes because I could see in the dark. Now I could see to the far side of the pond. Small animals had come to drink.

Clouds would occasionally pass the moon and cast shadows about. The owls could be heard, as well as the hawk, hunting and catching their prey. This is always how and where I restored myself. Just to stand on this hill and witness the world around me continue as it had so many times before.

This was God's way of telling me, "You are still here,

and a part of what I have created. You have to go on, to function and do your part as long as you are here. You must connect, contribute, and put back into this world all that you take from it. This is the way of survival for all." This is when I realized what I had to do. All was clear. I had always taken the love, security, compassion, safety, and harmony of my home, parents, and community. This is what I had to give back. I had to continue with the legacy my parents had passed on to me. I had to keep the secret alive, to let it grow and care for those less fortunate, to give back all that I so willingly had taken and enjoyed. I would be fulfilling God's design. I would also be keeping my parents alive. Their memory would always be there every time I used the secret. With this thought ended, the clouds broke away from the moon, and thousands of tiny lights spilled upon the earth, falling with mirrored impact upon the water: how beautiful. The tiny lights had a life of their own, each trying to do more than the next. My heart felt as though it would stop as I watched the large rays of light just under the moon. They had taken the faint shape of a cross. I realized then that God, because of His love and wisdom, had given me reassurance. I had sorted through my thoughts, and He was pleased.

How could I explain this place to others? They would surely think I had taken leave of my mentality. We have to realize that each of us has a way, a design, for our own needs. What makes sense to one will be lunacy to another, with both being right. It is up to individuals to identify and follow their own enlightenment.

I sorted through all of this, and years later, when I could understand what had really taken place that night,

The Journal

I did as most women do (especially the ones who keep a journal). I wrote verses. I am sure they will convey what I believe.

☆ ☆ ☾ ☆ ☆

I stand on the grass knoll
And revel in the peace I always experience in the
    water
I am alone
The soft music of the night resounds upon the
    wind
It caresses my cheek
My heart begins to pound
My eyes fill with tears
I remember they are not here
God fills this place and reveals to me my life
He gives me hope
He reminds me, for every question there is an
    answer
All prayers are heard
I stand over the water in prayer
With the moonlight coming down
I become one with its brilliance
I feel myself falling upon the wet ripples below
To glisten and bounce about, a part of a miracle
God had shown me the end of my beginning
To become one with Him
An ever faithful
Moon Dancer
One of His rays of light.

Moon Dancer

☆ ☆ ☾ ☆ ☆

I will continue now with what happened later that week, after Mr. Willard and Christina's visit. I did not mean to wander. I just had to share my emotional and spiritual self with you as well. Without these, you will never know the whole person.

Minnie and I discovered, the following Sunday, just what Mr. Willard and his daughter were about. We were to find that, indeed, as Minnie had said, "That lady is bad news." It was shortly before noon. I had just come in from the lumberyard and the dairy barns. I was not dressed for company, nor did I have a pleasant odor. Ladies in those days did not work freely on a farm and most certainly not attired, as I was, in men's clothing. This, over the years, has given Minnie and me a few good chuckles. But unfortunately, on that particular morning, it put me at a great deal of unease. Not only did Mr. Willard and his daughter call, they had also brought along several others: the reverend, along with some ladies from the church, and another lady I did not recognize. Minnie had shown them in and was about to come for me when I walked in on my way to the stairs. Having come from the back of the house, I had no idea they were there. I do believe we shocked each other equally. As usual, Minnie handled the situation with dignity, saying, "There you are, Miss Abigail. I knew you should be in shortly, finished with your morning duties. You have guests, and I have seen to tea." With this, she stepped back to allow me to speak. I stayed back and did not approach them. I said, "Please, if you

The Journal

will excuse me, I will remain here. As you can see, I am not properly dressed to receive guests. Is there something I can do for you?"

Reverend Mauldin nervously stood and said, "We are sorry to intrude, Miss Abigail, but I am afraid we have come with an urgent matter." At my puzzled look he continued, "I am sorry. This is not easy for me. Some of the ladies of the church and community, as well as Mrs. Forbes from the children's welfare agency, have brought it to my attention, and so has Constable Savage, that you are a minor without the proper care of an adult. I am sorry, child. I know you think you can manage this place because your father chose to let you believe it. It is another matter for you to attempt it without the support of him or another male."

Mr. Willard had interrupted, saying, "You are a mere child of seventeen. You would, in no time, lose all your father has spent his life working for. You must realize the futility of this venture. It is our responsibility, as your superiors, to protect you and look out for your interest. Your properties must be sold and the funds put into an account until you reach a legal age, as decreed by the courts. You will be educated in the finest of schools and be allowed to travel with proper supervision."

He could plainly see from my demeanor how this was affecting me. Even so, he did not stop, but continued with a vengeance. "Look at you. It is plain to see from your appearance and wildness of personality that you are in need of guidance and supervision. You are a lady, and at this moment you are anything but a lady. You look like a dirty farm hand. Had I not known who you were, I should have thought you a boy. I am sorry, but it is evident we were right to come here and intercede on your behalf."

Reverend Mauldin spoke once more. "Mr. Willard has agreed to top any offer made for your properties. This is why he accompanied us, to reassure you that you will receive a fair price, ensuring the stability of your future. Constable Savage visited your father's attorney and found that there was no will."

While he was speaking, Minnie had come to me, taking my hand. She prompted me to look at Christina and whispered that she had been all through the house while her father was speaking. She now joined him, wiping her hands and shaking her head. She had no remorse for me. At that moment, I realized that she wanted my home and all that was mine. She would do anything to obtain it.

Mr. Willard began to speak again and rather loudly, "The courts have a legal obligation to intervene in the best interest of a minor. We do not need your permission in this matter. You, Miss Duffin, will do as the law dictates. I suggest you prepare yourself. After the meeting Monday morning at eleven o'clock, you will be allowed to stay in my house until you are placed in a proper establishment appointed by the courts."

☆ ☆ ☾ ☆ ☆

I looked at all of them, and drawing on my courage, I thought of how Mother and Father would have handled this. I was surprised by my actions. I slowed down everything about me: anger, fear, and resentment. With

The Journal

as much dignity, grace, and poise one can possess, in men's clothing with cow manure all over them, I stood straight to my full height of five feet six inches and calmly said, "You will not sell my home. You will not take over my business, and you will not send me off to a boarding school so that 'lady' can turn my family's home into a disgusting appendage of her personality."

I then turned and began to ascend the stairs as slowly as possible. I envisioned my mother doing so on many occasions. In that moment, I could almost feel her beside me and hear her whisper, "Well done, my child, well done."

Mr. Savage approached the stairs, leaning in, looking up at me and speaking low, said, "I am sorry, Miss Abigail. If it were up to me, you know you could stay here." Then seeing how unresponsive I was, he turned to Minnie, saying, "Please, would you have her at the hearing on Monday?" He then turned to leave. I thought he looked a broken man. I now know, and I am sure a part of me was aware then, he was telling the truth. Reverend Mauldin said, "Please, child. We are only trying to do what is best for you." I could hear the others saying their good-byes to Minnie. Through all of this, Mr. Willard had been talking forcefully and rather loudly. I could tell by his tone he was a man used to getting his way. When I reached the top of the stairs, I turned and escaped into my room. As I closed the door I could hear him say, "Eleven, Monday morning, Miss Duffin; you had better be there." I never hesitated or acknowledged that I had heard either of them. Later, Minnie had relayed to me, "That woman stood beside him with a smug, haughty smile. As he spoke, she beamed all the more."

I stayed in my room for the rest of the day. I washed away the farm from my body, but nothing could remove the fear that was consuming me. I tried to find some reasoning in all that had happened and was happening to me. Minnie recognized I needed time. This she gave me. I was slightly aware that the shadows moved about the room in varying positions. I never moved from my place by the French doors. They opened onto the balcony. I stayed just inside, lost in my thoughts. My eyes sought the tree where the grave of my parents lay and, in a search for peace, just beyond to the faint image of Sutters Pond. So many questions there were. How will I survive, not my physical self, but my emotional self? How could I continue when I had lost all that was dear and familiar? My background and loving parents had given me maturity beyond my years. I have since realized that most people my age would not have had the presence of mind to realize the depth of their loss. They would not have reasoned it through as I did. They would have accepted their fate. Those involved thought my life was being settled fairly and that they had carried out their Christian duty, or duty to society. All was as it should be; I would be taken care of. No one realized that with all that I had lost, they were taking the most important possessions I had. Those were my rights, free will, and my ability to choose. I was refused the right to decide the direction of my future. No human being should have that kind of power over another.

What possible effect could a few months have on my ability to function as an adult? What miracle would happen to me on my eighteenth birthday? Would I wake changed? Did I not now possess that same ability

The Journal

to function rationally? This was the conclusion I came to on that long, lonely afternoon. No matter their good intentions, they did not have the right to force me to relinquish all that I had known and, most importantly, myself. This is the day I chose not to surrender but to fight for my rights as a person, to have a say in what was to be the rest of my life. I vowed that day to myself and to God that I would forever fight for my rights and the rights of others who faced similar circumstances. This has been my life's purpose, a commitment I have never once regretted.

I had concluded that the real reason for this farce was the farm and my home. Christina Willard had a fancy for this place and had gone to her father, who would do anything for his very spoiled daughter. This was also his amusement in life, not the acquisition, but the acquiring. He loved the hunt. Then he could use the one thing he had grown to love most of all, the by-product of his wealth: power. With his power he chose to use the law to get what he wanted. I decided I would use the same. I would find a proclamation that would allow me to keep my home. I would have to be resourceful. They would not be expecting me to do anything. I would have the element of surprise.

If by chance I could not find what I needed from the library downstairs, there was also New York. There was little time to waste. I had to have the answer by Monday morning. Those who were taking care of the house must have thought I had taken leave of my faculties. I dashed down the stairs and into the library, banging the doors.

Before I continue, I must tell you here how all of this with the Willards came about. There are also a few surprises; one being that Christina was, in fact, the woman Carl's father had promised him to marry. When Carl had rejected the arrangement and left town, Mr. Willard had married her to Bernard Emerald. He had become a senator for the state of Vermont. He had gone on to do quite well for our state. I am afraid I never came to possess such a high opinion of his wife. The Willards were traveling to their summer place, which was just north of The Old Place. With it being closer to her home and on a hill, just the way she had always wanted, Christina begged he father to buy it for her. When they passed through town, Mr. Willard went to a lawyer for advice.

He was aware that lawyers knew everyone in town, as well as their business. He visited the office of John Forest, who just happened to be Father's attorney. My father had said it would look rather odd if we did not have the service of a lawyer, from time to time. This is also how I later came to have this information. Mr. Forest had assured Mr. Willard that our place was not for sale, to which Mr. Willard had replied, "Nonsense, everything is for sale with the proper amount of money or pressure." This he had said, with a smile. "I will see Mr. Duffin, and I am sure we can come to an understanding." Mr. Forest had cleared his throat and sadly informed him that that would be impossible. "He and his wife were killed in an accident. They are to be laid to rest today at The Old Place."

Mr. Willard had stood up and hitched his thumbs under his suspenders and said, "Well, this does simplify the matter, doesn't it? I am sure the family could use the cash in their time of need." This is when Mr. Forest

The Journal

had told him about me. He had replied, "She is just a child. What will she do with such a place? This is much easier than I first supposed." He proceeded to light a cigar and looked quite proud of himself. Mr. Forest had assured him that I would manage the place myself. He had reassured him that my father had allowed me to be taught the way of business. Mr. Willard had answered, "Nonsense, women are not capable of such an undertaking. They should do what they were designed for: care for a husband and have babies. This is their purpose." He opened the door and left saying, "You have been most helpful; I can now handle this myself."

Mr. Forest had told me later that he knew there was going to be trouble. He realized he was partly responsible. Knowing my father had no will, he could see I was in trouble.

The Willards had evidently gone straight on to the house and funeral. Christina had looked the place over during the service. How cold it must be for those who have no compassion. (Please forgive me, my way. I must elaborate occasionally.) My mind has way too much knowledge stored and so little time to sow the seed so that others can enjoy and profit from its harvest. I will continue with my search in the library for a way to keep The Old Place.

After entering the library, I stood perfectly still. For all my hurry, I was now blank. "Think, think," was all I could say. I took a deep breath and cleared my mind. "Facts—go over the facts. What was the common denominator?" Then it came to me, "No will, there was no will." Since it wasn't with Mr. Forest's office, it had to be with the New York office. I could not tell anyone. I had to keep the secret. I would have to get a message to Mr. Abrams. He was in charge of the office. It was then I realized, in my grief, I had not let them know of my parents' death.

I spent the next half hour composing a letter to Mr. Abrams. I apprised him of the deaths of my parents and the situation, as well as the urgency. I needed an answer. Did they have a will? If not, was there an answer to my problem? I asked if they could acquire the services of Mr. Wheeler, the private investigator. He could deliver the will or an answer to my dilemma. I would continue to search for an answer.

I had Sam drive Minnie and me to Burlington in Father's automobile. Father had let me drive it a few times, but I would never have taken such a trip on my own. We had to go far enough, as to not bring attention to what I was doing. We sent a telegram and returned home late. I stayed up the rest of the night looking for an answer.

After returning home around nine, I went to the library. I immersed myself in book after book. While searching for an answer to my predicament, I found there was a more eminent concern. There were few laws governing children, minors who had no voice in the decisions that were to alter the course of their lives. These children were at the mercy of adults. If the adults' concern lay more for themselves than the welfare of the children, the children would be the ones to suffer the consequences. My case was such. Mr. Willard was executing the situation to conform to his own interest.

I was blessed to be educated and of an age to know there was an answer for me. What about those who could not manage for themselves? I knew this was what

The Journal

I wanted to correct. I wanted to defend children in my situation. I wanted to be a part of the process to establish the laws that would ensure the supervision of the selection of people who would represent them. I realized then, mentally, I had become much older than my seventeen years. Mother, Father, and I had always talked through a difficulty and reached a decision. Now, I would have to make decisions alone. The child-woman had vanished. I could not survive if she were to remain. I had become a woman in one horrifying week. I had to manage for myself. After hours of searching, I discovered an answer: General Laws, section 28 states, "The age of majority in the state of Vermont is 18 for women and 21 for men." There was also General Law 3643:

> The woman in question would have a guardian appointed for her with the power to dispose of her estate (with the approval of the probate court). If she did not want this to happen, she could petition the court for a new guardian.

I was ecstatic. If this was true and there was no will, I could petition the court to appoint Minnie as my guardian. She was over the age of majority by two years. I was perplexed by the difference between men and women. With the convictions of most men in those days about voting and education for women, I was amazed we had liberties three years earlier than our male population.

I could not petition the courts until Monday morning. I resolved to be there as soon as permitted. I would accomplish all I could before the eleven o'clock hearing. I spent the next few hours preparing documents using examples from current books. I used words I did not fully understand, taking time to consider each one.

When I emerged from the library there were still shadows. The sun would soon be rising. I loved the morning just before the earth began to wake. I sat on the stairs, about six from the bottom. There I could see to the west as my world slowly became visible. I tried to hold back the sorrow as Little Tree began to emerge from the darkness, sheltering its new treasure. Would I ever accept this, my new life, one without those dear to me?

Minnie was by the fire when I entered the sitting room. She put down her knitting and leaned forward, waiting patiently. I handed her the paper and poured myself a cup of tea. After reading it, she leaned back with a sigh and said, "You found it; our prayers were answered." I placed my hand over hers, saying, "Is it all right? I did this before I asked." Minnie smiled her warm smile and said, "You know I will do anything for you. You are my family. You have done well, Abigail. This is perfect. I am so proud of you. Instead of giving up, you found an answer. Your mother and father would be very proud. They raised you well. I have a feeling you are going to be a great lady. You will make a difference." I was overcome with emotion and could not speak. I squeezed her hand as the tears welled in my eyes. I went out on the porch to regain my composure, then to tell Mother and Father all that had occurred.

I met with Mr. Foster, and he agreed to represent me. We filed the necessary papers with the courts. He shared his feelings of surprise at my ability to do the necessary research and find an adequate solution to my problem. He complimented me on my tenacity and was also pleased with how I had found the law pertaining

The Journal

to my situation and had put together a legal document. He expressed that he only wished I had come to him for assistance. With his help, it would not have put such a strain on me.

Early Monday morning, I was at the courthouse in Montpelier, which is the state capital of Vermont. I did not know it then, but this would be my first of many visits. I would have an office there in years to come, but I am getting ahead of myself again.

I have come to believe that God had His hand on the situation. I was to be the one to find the answer. By doing so, I had found my destiny and purpose for my life. Sure, I now understand that Mr. Forest would have done the same had I gone to him. The point was that I had also been able to do this, and if I could, then I would be far better equipped with a proper education. This is exactly what I did.

After filing the papers and being assured that in due time we would hear from the courts, we returned to Williamstown for the hearing. Minnie was waiting for us. She asked if everything had gone well. Mr. Forest had replied, "With this one in charge, we have to do well. I am impressed. In fact, I think I should have her in my office. I can certainly use her fine mind." That was a compliment I would always remember.

The time was ten thirty. We found our seats and exchanged general conversation. Fifteen minutes later Mr. Willard, Christina, and two distinguished looking gentlemen arrived, all with the appearance of self-importance. Mr. Willard ignored us completely, with Christina giving us one of her smug, contemptuous looks. After that, everything happened so fast it overwhelmed us all. Mr.

Hastings, Carl's father, arrived just as we were about to begin. He was an overpowering personality. He was more than six feet tall, large in build, and middle-aged. He carried himself as a man accustomed to having his way. He approached the judge, addressed him by name, and said, "I have just today been advised of this preceding. I am a neighbor of Miss Duffin and her late parents. I feel that my presence here is warranted as my property line ends where hers starts. If anyone is to purchase her property, it should be me."

Mr. Willard jumped from his chair, ranting out of control. The two men with him were trying to calm him down. I could not help but think they were both of the same breed. The judge restored order to the room and instructed them to not let it happen again or they would have to leave. He silently read the papers and then asked, looking at me, "You are Miss Abigail Duffin?" I answered, "Yes, sir." He asked, "Are you represented by counsel?" Mr. Forest stood and answered. "Yes, sir. I was attorney for Mr. Duffin and feel a responsibility for his daughter." He then asked if there was a will. Mr. Forest had said, "I did not make a will for the Duffins." The judge had then asked, "What is the age of Miss Duffin?" "She is seventeen. Her eighteenth birthday will be in two months. As this is such a short time, I ask that the court be lenient with their decision to sell the estate and place her in a foster facility." "I am sorry, but all decisions have to be based on the facts. She is now a minor," the judge replied. With his answer, both Mr. Willard and Mr. Hastings had smiles take residence upon their faces. I could feel a fury I had never known before. I stood, took a deep breath, and started to speak. Mr. Forest had taken

The Journal

my arm and was trying to get me to sit back down. I had said, "I am sorry, but I have to speak. Just because I am two months away from my birthday, you are all acting as if I do not exist, that I am not present. I have feeling and knowledge. I know what is happening here. I have full understanding now. I won't miraculously gain it in two months. I see no great miracle that will transform me once it is a fact that I am in my eighteenth year.

"I can think and reason for myself. In fact, just this morning, Mr. Forest and I filed with the courts in Montpelier. We asked to have Miss Perkins appointed my legal guardian." This is when the two men both broke out in protest again. Mr. Willard was yelling that I was a minor and should not be allowed to enter into any legal proceedings. Mr. Forest had explained he was the one who had filed and all was legal. I sat again, so confused. I had never felt so alone or such a loss of control before. It was my life, my home, and my future. All they wanted was to win.

I became detached from my surroundings and myself, blotting out the noise. I instinctively turned to the back of the room. It was more like my head stayed forward and my mind or inner self tuned. There stood Mr. Wheeler, and on either side of him were my parents smiling. I could feel them say, rather than hear, "Everything is taken care of. Be happy, my child." The image faded away. I was back to reality with all the confusion around me. Suddenly a commanding voice sounded from the back of the room. "Excuse me, perhaps I can be of some assistance." A hush came over the room. Everyone turned. My heart stopped for a moment, for there indeed was Mr. Wheeler. He looked straight at me, smiling. Then, stepping before the judge, he said, "My name is Frank Wheeler. I represent the firm of Abrams and Abrams. After receiving a most urgent message from Miss Duffin, apprising us of the unfortunate deaths of her parents, I proceeded in much haste to arrive here today. We wish to inform the court that Mr. and Mrs. Duffin did, in fact, make a will with all arrangements for their daughter stated emphatically. Due to the nature of its content and expressed instructions, the will can only be viewed by you, the judge." He then handed the document to the judge. After reading it, the judge said, "If there is another outburst, I will hold both of you in contempt of court. Is that understood? I find that there is a will, naming Miss Duffin sole heir to the Duffin estate with a provision. If she is a minor at the time of their death, Miss Minerva Perkins is to be named her guardian. I will share with you their words:

> *We entrust the welfare of our daughter to Miss Minnie, who has, in fact, become to our hearts our daughter as well. We know that Abigail will be loved and cared for as no other could. Thank you, Minnie, for all your love and devotion. Good-bye, our daughters, be well and happy.*
>
> *Your loving parents*

Minnie and I had squeezed each other's hands with tears in our eyes. She said, "I knew they would have taken care of you. You were their life." The judge looked up from the papers and said, "I find that the will and accompanying briefs are in order. It is my opinion that this case is closed." He then handed the papers to Mr. Wheeler and left the room.

The Journal

The noise became deafening. Everyone was talking at once. Mr. Hastings stormed out of the building. Mr. Willard and Christina were talking to their lawyers. Mr. Willard threw his hands up and shouted something I could not understand. They began to walk away with Christina grabbing her father by the arm. I heard her say, "But, Daddy, I want that house. You have to get it for me." Mr. Willard threw away her hand and said in a very aggressive manner, "You cannot have it. There is no way that I can get it." She snapped, "Just buy it." He yelled back, "It is not for sale, so I cannot buy it." They had left the building still arguing with each other.

Mr. Wheeler had introduced himself to Mr. Forest and escorted us outside. When we emerged from the building, I was surprised to see that approximately the entire town had been there. Most had shaken my hand and congratulated me. I was overcome. Such was my emotion that when I thanked Mr. Wheeler I even hugged him. He had tipped his hat and said, "You know that you can depend on me, Miss Abigail. Anytime you need me, I will be here. I had the utmost respect for your parents, and after the last occasion on which I assisted you, you now have my respect, as well. I will look into a few matters here, and when I am satisfied, I will be on my way. God be with you, child." With this said, he excused himself and was gone.

Mr. Forest was puzzled and said, "I did not realize that your father had another attorney." I had spoken, touching his hand, "Father was a very private man. He had great respect for you and your abilities. The need to maintain his privacy led him to manage some arrangements elsewhere. Please do not be offended." He had assured me he

95

Moon Dancer

was not offended, just surprised. I asked if there was any more we needed to do. He assured me all was in order. He advised me to continue with my life, and if Minnie or I needed him, he would be pleased to assist us.

Minnie and I were leaving town when she remarked, "There is your Mr. Wheeler. He just entered the land office." I had asked, "Which one?" There were two on the same street. She answered, "Baker and Tubbs." We looked questionably at one another. Of the two, they were the more questionable. "Now, why would he go in there?" she had asked. We were both very puzzled and hoped to soon find out. It would, however, be two weeks before we saw Mr. Wheeler.

As we had tea by the fire that evening, Minnie remarked, "Abby, so much has happened and so fast—very devastating situations. You have conducted yourself admirably. I am so proud of you, but I want to know. You look fine on the outside, but how are you on the inside?" I had assured her I was fine.

Somehow, I was slowly finding a way to be a day person and function, as I should. I would let the night person grieve, for one must grieve. It is a very necessary process. You must not stop it. If you listen to your body, it will guide you. This I continued to do, at first trying very hard, until it slowly became part of my day.

A week after the incident with Christina and her father, I went to see Mr. Forest. We had talked for about an hour. He had agreed to be my mentor, to advise me in my choice of educational facilities, to support and assist in any way possible. I was to assist him three times a week in his office. He felt this would allow me the opportunity to see if law was really my calling. Or, in his

The Journal

words, if it "just filled a need for that one occasion."

It had, over time, proven to be a real calling and indeed my vocation. Without the law, I would not have been able to serve my children, as well as others. I realize, as time had moved on, the law and some who practice have gotten a bad name. But I assure you, they are in the minority. You have to rely on your instincts, do your research, and make sound decisions. I was very fortunate to have known some of the finest in the profession. With and through their help, I was able to achieve much success in my lifetime.

The first quality they possessed was fairness and an open mind. Believe me, for a man, especially of power and prominence in the early to mid 1900s to listen and take seriously a seventeen-year-old woman was quite rare. Women were not highly thought of in those days in an educational field, especially law and politics. They both became my field of endeavor.

Mr. Forest was from our hometown, Williamstown. Mr. White, whom I would later become associated with when Carl and I opened the orphanage, was from Montpelier. Both Mr. Abrams were our attorneys from New York. They were much more involved in financial law and were most helpful in the legal aspects of opening the orphanage. Mr. White was in civil law, which involved adoption and human rights. Mr. Forest was more probate, will, and matters of inheritance and human rights. Through them, I became very balanced in law, possessing an ability to keep a level head in my dealings with and through the orphanage. I was dealing with human lives. I could not afford to be careless and uninformed. It was a full-time job in itself to stay current with the changes in the legal system, especially those that governed human rights. I have, even as my age has advanced, continued to keep up with the changing times.

I have, over the years, come to call Mr. Abrams Sr., Mr. White, and Mr. Forest "the three wise men," a nickname they were proud of. They remained very dignified when I used it. You could tell that modesty kept them humble, but they were very pleased. I always had stand-in fathers. I was never lacking in having my needs met. So many times I thought fate, God, or my father had set them up for me to encounter; just maybe it had been all three

Sadly, being much younger, I outlived them. Such is the way of life. I will never forget them. I remarked to Minnie one night as we reminisced, "If there should be a need for lawyers in heaven, I had all four corners covered: the three of them and myself." We had both laughed at the thought of a court trial in heaven. Minnie had said, "What a sight that would be. Don't start without me. You will just have to postpone it till I get there." We had both enjoyed the evening, with many more of no importance, really just for companionship and memories. When you reach my age, you start to see what a treasure you have when they are present. I am sure, by now, that you are thinking, *Will she ever tell us why Mr. Wheeler went into the land office?* When you are my age, one can get away with this. More patience is allowed for the aged. Thank God for that, although it should be allowed for all ages, at all times. Back to Mr. Wheeler. He had come by the house about two weeks after Minnie and I saw him go into the Baker and Tubbs office. He had asked Minnie if I was home. He wanted to speak

The Journal

with me. Well, even if I was in China, Minnie would have brought him in, such was her curiosity.

I was by the fire. It had been unseasonably cold in the evenings for mid-May. We always looked for any excuse for a fire. We had both so enjoyed a fire all of our lives. Minnie had shown Mr. Wheeler in. He apologized for just dropping by. I had assured him he was like family and welcome unannounced anytime (which he took me up on many times over the years). He informed us that he had been so angered by the actions of both Mr. Willard and Mr. Hastings, that he took it upon himself to investigate them both. Minnie and I shared an astonished look and sat forward as he continued. "Mr. Hastings I found to be a hard man. As men often remark, he has 'an axe to grind.' He is just, for no apparent reason, a very unhappy man. I could not find anything. He has one son, who left home without his father's permission. No one knows where." I had sat transfixed, not breathing, as he spoke of Carl. "His wife is, for all appearances, a calming force in his life. I could find no dishonesty in his business dealings. He just has not a heart. As for Mr. Willard, I am afraid the opposite is true. I checked back several years on land and business purchases. I found him to be a very busy man. Apparently, he has forced, swindled, or coerced many families out of their homes who, like yourself, had a prime piece of property he had taken a liking to. My personal opinion is that he really enjoys the hunt rather than the kill. Sorry, ladies, I guess I have spent too much time around men. I have forgotten my manners." I had assured him that Minnie and I had been around men all our lives, even some men who were not afraid to be themselves, and we enjoyed his colorful analogy. Well, that was the best thing I could have said. He acquired the biggest smile I had ever seen him wear and continued. "I found there were four such deals in the past few years. On further investigation three of these families wanted their homes back. The homes had been in their families for hundreds of years. Mr. Willard had turned them into hunting lodges and getaways for his family and rich friends." Mr. Wheeler took a deep breath and smiled a strange smile and said, "Where we differ are our motives. I want to see justice done. I feel this is why I am successful at my job. My motives are good and just. I have always believed that God will champion us when we are striving for good. I took the liberty, out of respect for your father and mother, to set in motion the circumstance that brought about an investigation into Mr. Willard's illegal appropriation of land through use of fear and threats upon three families in question. It will take a little time, but they will get their homes back." Mr. Wheeler had been right. In time, the properties were all returned to the rightful owners.

☆ ☆ ☾ ☆ ☆

I had stepped out onto the balcony adjoining my room. As I was reminiscing, the cold night air felt invigorating. There had been a heavy snow that day. All was white and beautiful. From my position on the balcony I could see over the expanse of the farm, the fullness of the moon illuminating the evergreens, and holly adding signs of color for the Christmas season. How at peace I felt. I was now truly, for the first time, a woman. I felt like a

The Journal

woman. I had managed, with God's love and guidance, to keep my home, to pursue an education, and work toward the bar exam. Passing the bar exam would be the proudest day of my life. I did not, not once, have to wish my parents would be there, for I knew they would. I could feel them everywhere, in all that I did. I knew they were proud of me, and I must admit that I was quite proud of myself as well. Now, I was about to embark on a career in law. At the age of twenty, what I wanted to do was make a difference in the world, but I did not know how I was to accomplish this. I knew that God would reveal all to me in due time. I stood against the cold with my arms wrapped around me. I looked out toward the pond off in the distance. As always, my heart would swell at the thought of Carl. I had never stopped thinking of him. He was still as much a part of my life now as he was all those years ago. Yes, I was a child then, but in many ways a mature child. I had been tutored and nurtured. I was allowed to grow and mature in a natural way. This is how Carl had been to me as well. I had allowed him to grow along with me. Every time I looked at the pond, he was there in my mind. I had changed much, but also was the same. I did not take an interest in any of the young men that I had met. Carl, I knew, would be the only man for me. If I was to never see him again, then so be it. I would survive, for God in His wisdom had a plan for me. I had to trust in Him, as I always had.

What would Carl be today? How did he look as a man? He would be twenty-six now, in his prime of young manhood. I knew he had to be a fine-looking man now. I tried to see him as he would look today, but that boyish face was always there. Where had he gone from

Moon Dancer

here? What was he doing? How had be gotten by? I felt he was all right, that he was happy. The first few months after he went away, however, I knew he was not all right. I knew he was in trouble. The feeling had come over me the third day after he had gone. An intense pain and panic had passed over me. I had fallen to my knees and prayed as I had never prayed before. I knew he was in trouble. He was hurt, but I also knew God would care for him. Slowly, a little each day, the feeling began to fade. I was sure he was getting stronger. I never again felt that kind of feeling. There have been many occasions over the past years when I was prompted to pray for him, and I did. Somehow I was sure he was in need of God's help. As I stood there in the beautiful night, with the moon full, I prayed for Carl yet again, hoping for him to have a merry Christmas and be happy. I ended my prayer, as I always did, saying, "Someday, please, come back to me. I will never love another. This boy, in my mind, who has grown into a man, is somewhere out there in the vastness of our world. Find your way home, my Carl. I am still here waiting for you, now and always."

The cold had taken over, and I had to move inside. As I closed the French doors, I rested my head on the glass and closed my eyes. Lately, the woman feelings had slowly begun to come over me. I could feel Carl's arms around me, and my body ached for him. I was not sure how I could recognize this feeling. There had only been the one embrace on the day he said good-bye. Not having my mother to talk with, I assumed that one's body had a mind of its own in these matters. I remembered once my mother had said, "Abby, you are starting to grow into a beautiful young woman. Now is when you

The Journal

are going to have to listen to your mind as to what is right or wrong, and not to your body. You have choices to make. You are not living for a moment. You are to live a lifetime. Act that way." This I had always tried to do.

On the day of my parents' funeral, when I asked Minnie, "What shall I do without them?" Her answer to me had been right. She told me to listen with my heart and mind and the answer would be there. "You will always be able to hear them, if you believe." It seemed Minnie was always right. She was only two years older than me, but sometimes she appeared to be so much more. Even now, she was downstairs getting the house prepared for Christmas Eve dinner, my first meal at home for quite some time now. With me having been away at school, graduation, and preparing for the bar exam, Minnie had been there for it all. I will never forget my Minnie. How would I have survived without her?

I have come to realize that when these feelings of wanting and needing Carl came over me, I would make my mind move to thoughts of the world. But this night I felt it was all right to want and need him. Somehow I knew, somewhere, he was thinking of me. I stayed wrapped in my thoughts for some time. As I continued to dress, I thought about how there was, as almost always, just Minnie and I for the holidays. My friends were with their families. All the same, Minnie and I did Christmas right. We dressed ourselves up, as well as the house. We made it a tradition, for someday I had hoped to fill this house with lots of love and laughter.

At that moment, I could see Mother and Father at the top of the stairs kissing. She pulled away, ran down the stairs, and hid behind me. My father followed her;

Moon Dancer

all of us were laughing as they both tried to use me to hide behind. I smiled, what a wonderful memory. How fortunate to possess a mind, such a wonderful tool, for the past as well as the future.

I finished my hair. I had chosen to wear it down, and I wove long, thin red and green satin ribbons through it to loosely pull it back. They showed up well in my dark hair. I put on a long, heavy velvet dress of deep forest green, as it was cold. The green was festive. The full skirt hung straight, swirled lightly when I walked, and kept my legs warm. I stood back and looked at my reflection. I so much looked like my mother. I was taller than she by some two or three inches. She had been only five feet four inches. My father was almost six feet tall. He had passed some of his height on to me. My hair was dark like Mother's, but had a slight burnished copper to it that would sometimes catch the light. I like that as well. There again, Father was a little on the blond side, and I felt he had given me the golden glow. Hoping I was not being too vain, I felt I had grown into an attractive young woman. Then I realized, with such beautiful parents, I guess I could count myself blessed. I swirled about looking at my reflection, feeling very festive. I was in the spirit of the holiday. There was a knock on the door. I answered. Minnie opened the door. I was about to comment on the dress. On seeing her face, I stopped and looked questioningly at her. Minnie said, "There is someone here to see you. He is in the drawing room. He asked me to tell you that Carl Hastings is here to call for you." When Minnie saw the look on my face, she eased out of the room, closing the door.

I stood in total disbelief. He was here. He had come

The Journal

back. All those years of waiting were over. I could not move. I was at one with the floor. The only thing racing was my mind. He was downstairs. How would we be with each other? Would those feelings be there? Had I made them up? Would he be alone? Was he married? Finally, I stopped myself and pulled my thoughts together, along with my self-control. I opened the door. Minnie was there, as I knew she would be. I said, "Please, tell him I will be down in a moment." She asked if I was all right. I assured her I was. Minnie disappeared down the stairs. I took a deep breath, stretching myself to my full height. Then I smoothed my dress and lifted my hair back into place behind me. Leaving my room, I looked ahead and thought I could see my parents at the top of the stairs holding hands, smiling, and motioning me to go. This I did. I started down the stairs and stopped. Carl came out of the drawing room. He stood with his hat in his hand. As our eyes met, those long years were gone. All of the little fears and uncertainties disappeared. He was still my Carl. What a fine man he had grown to be. I, once again, began to descend the stairs to walk to him. He grew larger and larger. He was at least six feet six inches tall and weighed about 230 pounds. I could not believe how he had changed. At the same time, he had stayed that same young man I had known. His eyes and his smile—my Carl had come home. I will never forget that Christmas

    When I reached him, he put out his arm and with a beautiful smile gave me a slight bow. I took his arm, and we walked to the front door. Carl removed my cloak from the wall hook. He placed it about me and put on his coat and hat. He escorted me out to the sleigh that was waiting at the foot of the steps. He reached down, lifted me effortlessly, and placed me in the sleigh. He wrapped me in the blanket snugly. Then he came around and climbed in and took the reins. Off we went into the night. I had no idea where we were going or why. I did not care, for my Carl was home and I knew in my heart he would never leave me again.

The night was alive. Everything around me was intense: the sounds, the movements, the moon, the stars, and the snow. The trees in their winter dress were larger, more beautiful. The feel of him next to me, emotions that had lain dormant for so long were awakening now, what a wonderful gift. God truly was a mastermind. He had thought all of this through. He had known all was to match and come together in soulful harmony. God gave us an awareness of the things to come and a peaceful patience to wait to enjoy all of it, not to rush, for there can only be one all-consuming love. This was our first realization of the newness of a man and woman about to embark for a lifetime, for forever. This only will be once. We may love again, live again, have another life, but we will never have this again. We came to a stop on the hill overlooking the pond and our place, where we had met so many times. We had shared so many dreams. Carl had talked through his life and problems. This was where two very young and immature people had tried to solve an unsolvable problem, on a hill in Vermont, overlooking a pond, not realizing that the problem had to be resolved far from here.

Carl reached down and picked me up in his arms. As we moved from the sleigh, my arms, with a mind of their own, went around his neck. He looked into my eyes,

The Journal

smiled, and said, "Hello, my beautiful Abigail." Then his lips met mine, and the whole of my world righted itself. Then and there, the last piece of the puzzle fit into place.

I had never been kissed before. Carl and I never again shared a kiss quite like that one; I will never forget its magic. I am not sure how long it lasted, seconds or minutes. As he gently put me to the ground, I looked up at his face. This man I saw before me loved me. It was in his eyes, in the way he held me. I could not believe he was here. He put his hand on my face, looked into my eyes, and kissed me again, gathering me up into his arms. We held on to each other; all these new feelings, new emotions I was experiencing for the first time were overwhelming. Carl pulled himself back, and we each tried to gain control of our emotions. He said, "I asked in town if you were still here, if you had married or were promised to someone. They said you were not." I put my hand on his face and said, "They did not know that there has always been someone. I have been waiting for him to come back to me." Carl said, "Can you forgive me for those years?" While touching his face, I said, "I already have."

He went down on his knee, reached in his pocket, and pulled out a green velvet box, just like my dress. He opened it and held it out to me, then said, "My Abigail, would you be my wife? I promise to never again leave you. I will love and care for you until the end of my days." As I looked at his face, the moon shining about us as day, I knew we would share the rest of our lives together—all of it, the good, and the bad. We would love. We would always have love.

"Yes," was my answer. I went on my knees as he placed

a beautiful ring of diamonds and jade upon my finger. He brought it to his lips and kissed my ring and finger. "Never remove this to leave me. I will never be able to live again without you. Leaving you, a child-woman, I could, for I knew the time was not right. Now we are right for each other. I can never again leave." He gathered me once again in his arms and kissed me. We were lost in each other for a time. We rose from our knees, and Carl walked me to the bluff. We stood looking out over the frozen pond. He asked, "How many times have you come here since that day?" I looked at him, and it came to me. I said, "It was today, Christmas Eve six years ago today, that you left." Carl smiled, "How appropriate to return on the same day." I answered, "Yes, so many times I have been here. Nighttime is when I like to come the most, to be with you, to work out my problems. To be with God, to talk to Him." Carl said, "Abby, I am so sorry about your parents. I wish I had been here for you." I touched his arm and said, "You had your own problems to work through. Are you all right with that now?" He said, "Yes, I am now a grown man with my own life. My father can never touch me again. I will be amicable with him, for my mother's sake. I wish her no pain. I will go to her when I leave tonight. I wanted to see you first. Abby, I was so hoping you would say yes." He hesitated and gave a grin. "I made the arrangements for the wedding." I smiled at his shyness. He continued, "Will you marry me tomorrow, on Christmas Day? I know how much you love Christmas. What a wonderful way to start our life, the birth of our life together, on the day of the birth of Christ." How wonderful, to have such a warm and compassionate man ask to share your life.

The Journal

My answer had been and would always be yes. When I said yes to the wedding, he held me once again, telling me how he would come for Minnie and me in the morning. He had reserved the church and the minister for after the morning services.

I placed my hands upon his chest. He took hold of my shoulder. I looked up at him with a soft laugh, pushing upon his chest, and said, "I cannot believe how big you have gotten. I knew you would grow to be tall and would have changed, but never did I expect this." He asked shyly, "Are you disappointed, or do I frighten you?" I looked up at him and let my hands move to his face. "I am not disappointed at all, and I could never be frightened of you. You have a good heart and a kind soul. That has not changed about you." I rose up on my toes to meet his lips. He gathered me in his arms and lifted me off the ground, literally as well as mentally. We shared our time together, holding hands and sharing a hug, occasionally kissing each other. We walked along the same paths as we had those years before. We were both content to just be together. We knew we would have a lifetime together to speak of those years: what he was doing, what I was doing. For now, we were content to just be with each other. We walked to the sleigh, and Carl once again picked me up and put me in. When he had wrapped the blanket about me, I placed my hand on his cheek and said, "If this is a dream, I will never wake." Carl took my hand and kissed my ring finger and said, "This is not a dream. This is real, my Abigail. I shall still be here tomorrow and all of the tomorrows to come."

When he walked me to the door I asked if he would come inside. He said, "Tomorrow I will, Abby. I will never leave again. There are two women I love. I am looking at one, and I have to go see the other one now. I want my mother to be there for our wedding. I am not sure how this will turn out with my parents. I will let my mother do as she can, for she is my father's wife. She has to do whatever is best for her. I will take what she can give. I do not want to cause her any suffering. He is out of town until late tomorrow afternoon. I am free to see her at home tonight. I will have my meeting with him another time." Carl kissed me good night and opened the door. I went inside, and he said, "I will see you tomorrow at eleven." He smiled and winked, whispering, "Mrs. Hastings."

I could only stand in a trance. Part of me wanted to run after him, to not let him out of my sight. The other half reminded me that I had patience. I had used it for six years. I had to use it now. He had other obligations. His mother had also been waiting for his return. She had grieved for him and deserved to be put at peace. He was doing the right thing. There was tomorrow. We would be together tomorrow. I stood with my back against the door for a moment, drained of my energy.

Minnie eased out into the foyer, seeing I was alone. She almost ran to me. She took my hand and asked, "Are you all right? You are frozen. Come in by the fire." I had still not spoken. She set me in my chair by the fire. Kneeling in front of me, she asked again, "Are you all right?" I looked at her and said, "Yes, Minnie, for the first time in many years, I am all right. Minnie, I am sorry I did not tell you about Carl. I just could not. We met by the pond when I was twelve, and we became friends. When I was fourteen, Carl left because of his

The Journal

father." As I told her the story, she stayed where she was. She sat on the floor, held my hand, and listened as the entire untold story spilled from me. I had held it in for so long. It felt good to express myself, to share with my friend, my family. "I believed he would return one day but was afraid to tell my story, feeling that if I did, it would not come true. When you said his name tonight and he was here, I was stopped. My world just stopped. I could not believe it. Minnie, he asked me to marry him. I said yes. The wedding is tomorrow. He has already made plans for the church and the minister. He will pick us up at eleven." Minnie had looked at me with a question. I asked, "What?" She said, "I will stay here and prepare the house and Christmas dinner." I in turn said, "You will do no such thing. You will go with us, and Mrs. Hart will prepare the house and food. You can arrange it, if you like, but she will prepare it." I jumped up, grabbed her hand, dragging her up the stairs. I said, "We have to find Mother's wedding dress. I hope it fits me."

We went to the attic where Mother's trunks were. As we entered the room, an unusual feeling came over me: a warm, calm feeling. I could have sworn my cheek was kissed. Seeing the expression upon my face, Minnie asked, "What is it? Why are you looking like that?" I told her what had just happened, and she smiled and said, "Just maybe you *were* kissed."

The wind had begun to blow, causing the feeling of a gentle swaying motion. I went to the window that looked out over the barn and Little Tree. The snow had again started to fall. Soft blowing flakes were whirling around as if dancing. "How beautiful it is, Minnie," I had said. She answered, "So is this." I turned and gasped. She

Moon Dancer

was holding my mother's wedding dress up for me to see. It was just beautiful. Not pure white, an off-white, linen gauze, with hand-made crocheted lace. Layer upon layer. I was sure it was the finest lace and from England. I gently touched the dress, afraid it would fall apart. Minnie said, "Here, let's try it on." I came out of my Christmas dress and slipped it on. Minnie buttoned the back and the sleeves, from elbow to the wrist. I stood with tears running down my face. I could not speak. As Minnie placed the veil on my head, I whispered, "Thank you, Mother. It is just beautiful. It fits like it was made for me. Thank you both for loving me." A soft wind seemed to blow gently, moving the lace and my hair. Minnie said, "They are pleased also. Did you see the lace? It seemed to move. If it would ever be possible for them to come to you, it would be now."

Minnie had uncovered an old floor-length mirror. I could not believe my eyes. This stranger, this happy beautiful woman, could she really be me? I had always heard that love is the most powerful emotion in the world. It had truly transformed me. Minnie was crying and wrapped her arms around me. She said how happy she was for me. "You and Carl make a beautiful couple. I am so glad he came back to you." "So am I, Minnie, so am I."

☆ ☆ ☾ ☆ ☆

Christmas morning came bringing a beautiful, still day. There was enough sun for beauty, not too bright, upon the snow. I threw on my boy clothes, as Minnie had

The Journal

come to call them. I ran down the stairs and out the side door, straight to Little Tree. I sat down upon the grave and happily told my story, wishing my parents a merry Christmas. I went to look for Mr. Thompson. He brought me up to date about the farm and showed me the new stock and the babies that had recently been born. I wished him a merry Christmas and rushed to the house. Minnie was in the kitchen with Mrs. Hart who, when she saw me, began to cry and tell me how happy she was for me. Minnie smiled slightly and said, "I hope you do not mind. I had to tell Mrs. Hart, for I wanted her to know how special this day is." I took her hand and touched my cheek to hers and said, "You did exactly as you should have." I turned to Mrs. Hart, thanked her for her congratulation and for making the preparations on such short notice. She assured me that all would be ready upon our return and what an honor it was for her to prepare for our wedding celebration.

The rest of the morning was a haze of activity. At ten thirty Minnie knocked on my door, entered, and came rushing up to me. Taking my hand she said, "I will help you with your dress and hair, if you like." I assured her I would. When we finished, we both stood in silence, looking in the mirror. Minnie squeezed my hand and said. "No, don't you cry, for we shall both look a fright when your Mr. Carl arrives." At that moment, we both heard a noise from outside. She and I smiled at one another. I said, "How wonderful to have you here, Minnie, through all the moments of my life. You will never know what a blessing you have been to me. I love you, and I shall always love you." We embraced, and she told of her love for me. I held her by the shoulders and looked her in

113

the eyes as I said, "I am today to marry Carl and make a wonderful life with him, here in this home that my parents brought to life by their love. We shall endeavor to do the same. I want you to know that while there will be change; you being my family shall not change. You shall always have a loving home here for as long as you live. You and Carl shall come to love each other as you and I." We had embraced for a moment. Minnie said, "I am so very happy for you, Abigail. You deserve much happiness in your life. I am honored to be here. I will always be here for you. This is my calling. I know I will never marry or leave. I am happy and doing what I want. Never worry for me, for my life is a part of The Old Place. Now, let's not keep Carl waiting. He will be a bundle of nerves." She squeezed my hand, saying, "Although upon seeing you, he will be anyway." She ran ahead of me, saying, "Wait, take a deep breath, then come down the stairs slowly. You will be a bride only once. Make it last. Make memories for a lifetime."

    I knew she was thinking of Carl seeing me come down the stairs, and I was later to realize that she was also thinking of me seeing him. I caught my breath and let it live in my body for a time. As I gazed upon the man before me, I remembered how he had left a mere boy and was now a man. There was about his eyes the kindness of a gentle soul. There was life, also. I could see the world had touched him as he had lived apart from me. Also, he had not lost himself during this time. I was so proud of him, even not knowing where or what had been his life. I knew it was a life to be proud of. In time, we would share with each other those separate lives. We would continue on, making a life with and for each other.

The Journal

That night for me has been as two different versions, one of clarity, vision, and understanding, and one of a surreal fairytale, opaque glimpses of two shadows realizing love. Without clarity, I would have forgotten walking up to him. How we stood mesmerized, afraid to move. He touched my cheek and said, "All the treasures I have found are too pale compared to you, for you are my treasure and will be until I am no longer here. I will always do everything within my power to make you shine." He was true to his word. He devoted his life to me, my purposes, everything I strived to accomplish. He was my strongest supporter. Minnie was always there, as well. Carl never left her out. They never passed a cross moment of words or jealousy. Each had their place in my heart. Neither of them was ever threatened by the other.

We stood for a long moment with his hand on my face. Slowly, he leaned over and kissed me ever so softly on the cheek. Caressing my face with both hands, he whispered. "Shall we begin our new adventure together?" I was trembling. I could barely hear my answer, "Yes." I had never before, nor since, seen such a beautiful man. My soul was so touched by his. He was beautiful inside and out. He remained so all our life together.

Carl gathered me up in his arms, and taking care of my dress, he turned and asked Minnie, "If you would be so kind as to open the door, I will make this woman my wife." There was laughter all around. For the first time, I noticed Mrs. Hart, her two daughters, Mr. Thompson, his son Drew, and Sam, who had grown up with Carl and was to be his best man. They were so happy for us. Carl had, with his great stride, taken the porch and lawn in very few steps. As he passed Minnie, he asked her to wait on the porch. He placed me in the sleigh, wrapping me in quilts of lace and satin.

On seeing the surprised look on my face, he said, "A special day should have special surprises." Having tucked me in, he once again returned to the porch. All were there smiling and laughing. Even the dogs were being quiet, looking like they too were smiling. Carl swept up Minnie, as well. I remember thinking how like a feather she appeared as he carried her and placed her in the sleigh. At her startled expression, we all laughed hysterically. We were then on our way. Such a beautiful day it was. There shall never be another quite like it. That is why I take time to share every moment of it with you.

The church was small, just the right size, sitting majestically on the side of a hill covered with snow and evergreens. The smell is still there for me, clean, crisp, and full of green. The church bells were ringing as we approached. There were people walking, and others came by sleigh; all were waving and laughing happily as we came to a stop in front of the church. Carl deposited Minnie on the stoop and returned for me. Those moments were only for the two of us. He placed me down at the entrance. I turned and looked inside. A wonderland awaited us. The whole of the church was aglow. Hundreds of candles were burning. They twinkled and glittered. Flowers were everywhere. Every shape, size, and color. At the altar was a large arch covered with candles and rosebuds. Under the arch, back just a little, was my Christmas tree from home. It was all lit up. I was so surprised, I could not move. I looked at him, "How did you do this?" He replied, "With the help of dear friends. Your dear friends, Sam and Mr. Thompson, brought the tree while you

The Journal

dressed. The ladies of the Garden Club supplied the roses and flowers from their hothouses. Everyone brought all the candles they had. There is not another candle to be had in town. I wanted you to always remember today, my love." I replied, "I will, because with all the beauty and wonderment, there is the reality of you."

The organ had begun to play. Carl had let go of my hand and walked to the front of the church; taking his place, he turned. Minnie had handed me a beautiful bouquet of yellow and ivory roses. As I started to move down the aisle, I stopped and reached my hand to Mr. Thompson, for he had been Father's trusted friend. He had taken care of me as well as the farm. He had taken over all of Father's responsibilities and had been like a second father to me. I had not consciously realized this until that very moment. His startled expression was replaced by a knowing smile and a tear. He offered me his arm and escorted me down the aisle to stand before the minister. When the minister asked, "Who giveth this woman to this man?", I could hear the pride in his voice as he answered, "I do." I turned and kissed him gently on the cheek, "Thank you, Mr. Thompson." He had smiled, "My tomboy is now a lady." My heart feels like it will burst, even now, so many years later.

The moments of life are truly God's treasures. Do not rush through life and miss the treasures. They are so few as these. There are some moments that will only happen once. Carl and I made all of it last, every minute of it.

Carl had prepared the minister's lines for him. My heart was warmed at how thoughtful he was of me and my place in the community. He had the minister explain, in an impassioned way, how we had come to know one another (leaving out the parts about his father). The minister recounted all that had taken place, how Carl had waited for me as I had waited for him. Carl had worded it so well. There was now no doubt as to my status as a lady. He had saved my name and reputation that day. He changed a potentially damaging circumstance into a fairytale. Our story was told and retold for years to come; for that alone, I would have loved him. He was ever so kind and thoughtful. Until the end God blessed me greatly. Your mate is the most important aspect of your life, your earthly life. If God is the head of your spiritual life, all else shall fall into place. It is up to you to pace your life. Fill it with lasting moments.

We said the traditional vows for the church and the people. Both knew that we would save our true feelings for us, alone. Our eyes spoke volumes. Where the heart is concerned, words are not necessary. When the ceremony was over, Carl turned with me on his arm and, once and for all, put to rest another potential problem. He had simply said, "My wife, Abigail, and I invite all of you to our reception at our home. It was her wish to continue to live in the home and atmosphere of love her parents had provided for her. She and I shall strive to equal the love and devotion shared by Eliza and Reginald Duffin. May they rest in peace." He had thought of everything; and the beauty of it all was, it had come from his heart (which was just as big as he was).

When we had returned home, Carl deposited Minnie and myself once again on the porch. He moved the sleigh toward the barn where Sam met him. He gave the reins to him, stepped on the porch, put his arm around me, and we turned. We looked out toward the pond

The Journal

and exchanged a knowing smile. Carl had said, "Mrs. Hastings, shall we go and prepare for our guests?"

The rest of the day was a blur of activity. Gifts were everywhere. Wedding gifts, Christmas gifts, food, wine, and music. The organist from the church played Mother's piano with much reverence. I had to coax her to play. She was in awe of it. It was so old and beautiful. I assured her that Mother would be honored since she was not here to play for me. Then and only then did she agree to play. Never had the rooms of the Old Place been so filled. From that day forward our doors were always open to everyone. Carl was once again accepted into the community. His sincerity and open personality melted any rumors they may have heard.

No one ever spoke of the years he was gone or of the rift between him and his father, which always remained. They were cordial when they chanced to meet. Carl would have forgiven him and moved on. Sadly, not Master Hastings. He was a stubborn, hard man. His pride cost him a wonderful son and the opportunity to share his life.

Later in the evening, after everyone had gone, Carl set me by the fire and said, "I have one more surprise for you." I had remarked, "I do not think I can take another." He had turned at the door and smiled, "You do have just one more left in you, dear." With this, he was gone. Minnie entered with our finest tea service, placing it on the old English cherrywood tea cart. It was Mother's pride. At the smile and knowing look on Minnie's face, I inquired with a gesture. With this, her eyes went from me to the door. There in front of Carl was the most exquisite little lady. She was poise, beauty, and elegance

119

all wrapped in a veil of vulnerability. I instantly knew her to be Carl's mother, Winifred Hastings. He was so like her. He had his father's size and strength of will, but with the attributes of compassion, reason, and a love of God from his mother. He was truly a man with heart and soul. He would always command attention and respect. Carl ushered her forward. I stood as he introduced her. Minnie had silently left us. Over the next hour or so we forged a friendship that would last us the rest of our lives. We developed a relationship apart from his father, out of respect for her marriage. We let her set the rules. She loved her husband and her son. She would respect them both. She never would openly defy Mr. Hastings. He knew she saw us from time to time. He chose to look the other way, as long as she was not obvious. Carl and I had enjoyed many such evenings with Winna, as she asked me to call her.

After she had gone, Carl returned to me. He said, "Go upstairs and change into your boy clothes that Mr. Thompson has been telling me about. (We both smiled.) We will ride down to the pond." We both went to separate rooms at the top of the stairs. I went straight to the closet to get my things. There, hanging was the largest jacket I had ever seen. It was made of hide with a matching hat. I wrapped my arms around the jacket. The smell of Carl was about me. To this day, when I miss him, I wrap myself in that same coat, and I can still smell the scent of him.

I was standing at the top of the stairs when Carl emerged from the room that had been my parents'. I smiled. How they would like that, I thought. Carl stopped short and laughed so hard he had to sit down on the stairs. He told me that the sight of me that night was just as memorable for him as seeing me in my wedding dress. He said, "There you were in your boy clothes, with your long hair down all about you, that huge jacket hung almost to the floor, you had no hands showing and a hat that came down to your nose. No eyes or ears were showing, just lips. You just looked thrown away." I could just see him from under the hat. He gathered me in his arms and placed me on his lap. He kissed my nose and said, "You lighten my heart." He kissed me gently. We shared a knowing look for a moment. Then he said, "The moon will be full soon. Let's hurry." When we rode out over the fields, his arms around me, there was a gentle swaying. Blade was one of the finest Morgan horses in the area. He was Father's horse, and after that night, he became Carl's. They were magnificent together. One could but gaze upon them if they passed.

The moon was indeed full. Everything was so beautiful. The night was still, the snow heavy, but Blade traveled well through it. The trees were covered. The tall evergreens were the most beautiful. They were very majestic, with the moon reflecting back from the ice crystals on the branches like thousands of tiny lights. How magical the night was as we emerged on the knoll above the pond. We held our breaths, for the pond was alive with the moon. Most of the pond was frozen except for the middle. The tiny lights were everywhere. As we sat watching, I was once again reminded of the poem I had written. I recited it to Carl. When I finished, he said, "You are so right. You captured all of it in those words. Let's make a pact to forever, from this night forward, be `Moon Dancers'. I should like to think that, when my time comes, I would become one of God's rays of light and dance about, with a life of my own. Should I go first, I shall always dance for you." I have often thought back over that evening and his words. I will always believe that somehow, maybe not consciously, Carl knew he would go before me. I always remember him when I see the moon dancing on the water.

Carl helped me from Blade, then turned and faced me. "I know how much this place has meant to you. How you have come here for solace and strength. I have a strong tie here, as well. Those two young people will forever live here. Sharing your poem with me about this place makes it perfect for me to pledge my vows to only you in God's presence. To love, honor, care, and cherish you until my last breath. Then, I will wait for you on the other side when your time has come, for we are two halves. When fit together, we make a complete whole. I shall never again be complete without you. I love you, Abigail Hastings. Please share my love, my life, joys, and sorrows. I will always be faithfully yours."

I was so overcome I could hardly speak. I reached into my pocket and handed him a small tattered package. It was wrapped in Christmas paper. "It has gone under the tree every year since you left. I made it for you as a gift. I brought it to give to you the last time I saw you here. I did not get a chance." Carl opened it. There was a mall piece of red cloth in the shape of a heart. "You have always had my heart. I just kept it for you." We both cried and held each other for a long time.

When we reached the top of the stairs after returning home, Carl took my hands and turned me to him. The soft glow from the wall sconce allowed us to see each

The Journal

other. He said, "I want you to listen carefully to what I say and understand. You and I have been through a lot. We have been apart for a very long time. We are both secure in our love. My return last night, the wedding, my mother, the reception, all those people, it is all overwhelming. I want you to go to your room and me to you parents' room. We will wait until the time is right to be together. I want it to be special. Just you and I. Let's get to know each other as friends. I want to know of your life and your accomplishments. I also want you to know my life and me. We need to know what has made us who we are today. We have much to share before we can share true passion. We have waited this long, a little longer won't matter.

"We shall be the better for it. Not tonight, for that is what is expected, but whenever we are truly one and come together, no matter where or when, we will both know. Do you understand?" I answered, "Yes," and I did. We indeed became friends; we laughed, worked the farm, played, and went to church together. We got to know people that each of us, separately, already knew. Making our worlds one, he shared his six years with me and I shared mine with him. I was so moved by his stories. He became a man to me, not just the boy I knew. They both merged as one in my mind, one over the other. For this man I developed a new respect. He had made a decision about his life; instead of bitterness he had opened himself to the world. He had taken on the world, made a difference, and emerged a grown man. How I admired him; his life had moved me. I could see when I had spoken of my life with its trials and triumphs, he had been moved in much the same way.

Moon Dancer

I shared with Carl the story of the death of my parents and his father's past role in my life. I shared how others and myself saved the farm, the children, and all about my education. We truly became real to one another. Two months after we had married, I woke in the night. I was not sure why something was drawing me to the window. I looked at the clock. It was three o'clock in the morning. I listened. I could hear nothing. I could still feel something urging me to go to the window. I made my way and looked out. I could not see anything out of the ordinary. I put on a heavy robe and moved silently out onto the balcony. My breath stopped. There was Carl, just in front of Mother and Father's grave. Placing him in line with the view of the pond, he was in his boots and pants only. With snow everywhere, he held a huge saber in each hand and moved with the grace and fluidity of a ballet. His movements with the sabers were with precision and hypnotic. I could not take my eyes off of him. I had never seen anything so beautiful. Despite the snow and the cold, he was sweating. The moonlight made his skin glisten and shimmer. His hair fell across his face, which was so intense with emotion. He was lost in his own world. He was only unto himself. I thanked God for allowing me to secretly share this with him, for if he knew I was there, he would not have been the same. I did not move until he turned toward the moon and bowed. He stood with his legs spread apart and, except for his body breathing hard, was perfectly still. I silently went back to bed and dozed for a time.

I woke again and was wide-awake. I moved silently to the door, went out, and opened the door to Mother and Father's room. I pulled the covers back and lay down

The Journal

by my husband. I shall not share this with you. You are only to know that he had been right about us waiting. I never once regretted waiting those years or even the two months after we were married. My being able to secretly share this night in the snow was to let me know our minds had become one. Now it was time for our bodies to follow. There was magic that night and has been since. What a wonderful gift, memories.

☆ ☆ ☾ ☆ ☆

On the night Carl asked me to marry him, he explained some of the details of how he spent the past six years. The full story came later, as we grew in our newfound love and freedom with each other. He had indeed left on that Christmas Day after meeting me at Sutter's Pond. He had felt guilty about leaving me the way he had, with just a letter, but he knew, with his father's attitude, we could never be together. We were both young. I, being only fourteen, needed to enjoy my youth and get an education. At nineteen Carl was old enough to realize this. He was not sure if I would wait for him. He did the only thing he could do. He wrote me a letter, being as plain about his feelings and the situation as he could be. He had to take that chance. He knew that once he became a grown man with some life lived, then and only then would he be able to face his father. This he would have to do someday, despite the fact that his father was not a forgiving man. He hated leaving his mother, for she did not deserve any of this. She too was a victim. He made himself a promise that once a year at Christmas, he would notify her of how he was, and this he did. He could see no other way.

Carl had managed to earn a little money while he was away at school. He didn't want anything from his father. In preparation to leave, he took the money he had saved and bought his own clothes, suitcase, and travel items; he then walked the four miles to town. Carl bought a ticket to New York and boarded the 3:15 train, not to be seen again until six years later. He had lost himself in New York, for his father would look for him; he even hired private detectives.

It was only after he was on his own that he was able to discover who he really was. At home, his father orchestrated everything he did. He chose the schools Carl would attend, the kind of education he would receive, and the vocation he was to pursue as a man. Carl's free time was not even his. His father chose books for him to read and demanded his friends come from prominent families; Carl had to spend his summers with them. He lived nineteen years under total domination. His father believed he was only ensuring his son was never idle and that he would pursue an honorable vocation. His father's ideas were good and his motivation honest, but somewhere along the way his control over Carl became an obsession. Carl made a decision to never again allow his father to dictate the direction of his life. He knew that a man had to rule over his own destiny. Like his father, Carl was strong-willed and forceful. Rather than use these traits to challenge and confront his father (which would only hurt his mother), Carl decided he would go and choose his own direction. One day he would return not for his father, but for his mother.

The Journal

At the time, I understood why he left, but I was lost with no word or assurance of his well-being. I placed all in the only place I could: God's hands. Once I asked Carl why he had not, in some manner, contacted me. He answered, "I knew you would worry from year to year, waiting for that one letter. Since we had no assurance of a future, I chose to let life dictate our futures. I went on with mine, and by me not writing, you would go on with yours."

He had sought to lose himself in SoHo, the old China section of New York. On the night he arrived, Carl had learned a very hard lesson in a very short time, which would change his life forever. On his way to find a place to stay, he was beaten, robbed of everything, and left for dead. Had it not been for an old Chinese gentleman who found him, took him to his place, and cared for him, Carl was not sure what would have happened that night. Days passed and he grew stronger. The old gentleman's name was Quan-Yen. He was a dealer in art and ancient artifacts, primarily Chinese. He said to Carl, "I am always looking for museum pieces. One day I will find." His place of business, The Antique Jade, was located in SoHo. On his way home that night, he had found Carl. As time passed, he and Carl became friends. In reality, Quan-Yen became the loving/nurturing/caring father Carl never had. He began to teach Carl about his business and put him to work. Under his tutoring and patience, Carl grew as a man and as a person. Carl was surprised to discover he had an eye for art, as well. Carl was always able to choose the oldest and finest of pieces. This delighted Quan-Yen. In time, he was to send Carl to China and much of the Orient to procure rare pieces for the business. In fact, Carl was to serve Quan-Yen's wealthy clients who wanted certain pieces or just a rare beautiful piece for their home. Before meeting Carl, Quan-Yen would personally assist his high-end clients. He would be received into their home, talk with them, tour their home, and develop an understanding of their taste to know exactly what would blend with their style. One day he said to Carl, "I am getting older and do not travel as well on the boats as when I was young. The voyage has become a chore, not so much a pleasure anymore. I want you, Carl, to take over this part of the business for me." Carl accepted his proposal.

Carl found he reveled in his new freedom and was fascinated with this whole new world he was discovering. How fabulous the world was. This is when he realized how closeted and totally confined he had been all his life. How unfair that all of these wonders were kept hidden from him; that he was not given a choice. Now he could understand what being incarcerated must be like. Only most prisoners had at least known freedom before: he never had. Sometimes, he felt like a child in his learning experience.

The Sea Wind was a beautiful vessel. It was not as big as some, but not small. She sailed smooth and sure. Her captain was John Chandler. He was a rugged man, admired by all who knew him and avoided by those who did not. Chandler and Quan-Yen were to be lifelong, trusting friends. Under their guidance, Carl, the tall, thin sapling of a boy, grew into a solid giant of a man. With Quan-Yen's help, he learned to protect himself. He taught him the old ways of the art of self-defense. Quan-Yen would joke and say, "With the size you have

The Journal

become, you only need to look mean with those eyes, and all will run."

Chandler would put Carl to work in the hold loading and moving boxes. He did this for one reason only, to help Carl build muscle: boxes for arms and upper body, and the swaying of the boat for the lower body. Chandler would watch and smile, and nod his approval. In time, Carl's body became rock-solid. No one bothered him ever again. His mind was filled also, with knowledge.

The Sea Wind was also his teacher. She showed him people, places, and events. How wonderful the world was. He learned also of the world's sadness and how unfair it can sometimes be. Some can have so much, while others suffer and have so little.

☆ ☆ ☾ ☆ ☆

Carl was with Quan-Yen two years by the time he had his twenty-first birthday in 1917. He was happy and well adjusted and had taken an interest in life and the world news. Traveling extensively as he now did, he became aware of the unrest in the world. On his travels overseas his approach to finding art was the exact opposite as in the United States. His business dealings were in the poorer sections, the reason being that most people having pieces of art were unaware of their value. He still would cater to the wealthy, but found a new market in old rare art from the poor who were holding on to pieces handed down from generation to generation while not being aware of their value. The poverty always touched him. He always wished that there was something he could do, but with

129

Moon Dancer

so much everywhere, how could he possibly make a difference? On the night of his twenty-first birthday he was to find out.

Carl had just returned from China, where he had discovered a very rare Ming statue in China's Yellow River Valley, not far from Siam. The statue had been in the owner's family for many generations. An early ancestor had stolen it after the fall of the Ming dynasty, which ruled during the fifteenth century. The family had little knowledge of its history or value. Situations like these are why Quan-Yen taught Carl to comb the villages and poor sections of China. Carl loved it when he saw the look on the people's faces when he paid them for the pieces. He always paid them a fair price. He knew in some small way he was helping these families take better care of themselves. Yes, he knew that they were lacking in education and would not use the money as wisely as they should, but you cannot change everything, and not much overnight. He took comfort in the things he could change.

Quan-Yen had been ecstatic when Carl placed the Ming statue in his hand. He told Carl of how his family was descendants of this dynasty. His ancestors had tried unsuccessfully for generations to locate the statue. As a small boy, he had learned of the existence of the statue and the story of its loss. He had hugged Carl and became overwhelmed with emotions. Carl had left him alone in his room and returned to his.

Later that evening, they had their meal together and Quan-Yen had given him a birthday present, a very fine pair of sabers, which he had traced back to fifteenth-century China. The sabers were reportedly owned by a

The Journal

mighty warrior of that century. That each had received gifts that evening from fifteenth-century China pleased Carl and Quan-Yen. When they retired to sit and talk, Quan-Yen had another surprise for him. He told Carl of the real purpose for his work and travels. Now that Carl was twenty-one and in command of a very fine education, he could help Quan-Yen in his other work. Quan-Yen revealed that he was also employed by the U. S. Government as a messenger. With the war going on (World War I), the State Department needed information on the allied activities. There were spies all over Europe, China, Russia, and Germany. Carl was well known for his travels by the persons who would have been suspicious. For two years now there was nothing on him. No one would suspect him. Quan-Yen only wanted him to become part of the war effort if he wanted to be. Conventional methods for information could not be used. Secrets had to be smuggled in and out with the utmost care. Times and dates for Allied offense had to be obtained and relayed to the proper authorities. He had also told Carl that if he were caught, the consequences would be death.

Just two years before, about the time Quan-Yen found Carl beaten in SoHo, an English nurse named Edith Cavell had been captured and subsequently executed by a German firing squad for helping Allied soldiers escape to the Dutch border. She lost her life but she had saved two hundred men over several months' time. He also told him that the French had just captured a Dutch dancer by the name of Mata Hari on charges of being a part of the German spy networks. It was only a matter of time before she was to be executed, and she eventually was.

Moon Dancer

"I do it for my country. America is my home now. Yet my ties are still strong with China. I fight for the U. S. My honors are strong and proud. I would sacrifice my life for my cause and country.

"You have much to lose if you fail and much to gain if you succeed. This is your choice." He had left Carl to think about all he had told him. Carl's answer had been yes. He had entered the war effort through Quan-Yen. He was his only contact in the States. For four years he passed on information to his contacts overseas, never meeting with the same person more than once. When he returned to the States, Carl would then pass the information to Quan-Yen, and months would go by before Quan-Yen would let him know what it achieved for the war effort. Carl found great comfort in knowing he had helped in winning the war.

Carl was hesitant about giving even me any information of his activities during this period of time. He would tell me that he had conditioned himself to lock away all he did and the information he had. Even after all this time, it was hard for him to open up and talk freely about it.

One of the stories he shared with me, I must pass on. I only tell of these things because, when this journal is read, we shall both be no more on this earth. The telling of his life then, as much as he could share with me, I will share with you, for I am so proud of my Carl. Such a good man, one of God's finest. Yes, the story. Forgive the ramblings of an old lady. Carl, for the most part, would relay messages from one continent to another. On rare occasions, he was asked to do more. The first time was when Lenin took Czar Nicholas II and his family to

The Journal

Ekaterinburg. The czar's conduct during World War I was questioned by the fourth Duma, elected in 1912. This was the lower house of the Russian legislature. They were seeking more power for themselves. This helped bring about Nicholas' abdication in March 1917.

In 1918, the Bolsheviks murdered Nicholas and his family in a cellar at Ekaterinburg. The Bolsheviks were later called Communists. Carl's mission was to locate the czar's family after his loss of power. They had left by train on their way to New Mountain City. Carl had been in Ekaterinburg when they were murdered. He and the men he was traveling with, although they stayed separated from each other, were to get the family out before the Bolsheviks could get to them. Our government wanted to keep them alive so political unrest in Russia would remain. Lenin wanted the czar dead. If the family disappeared and could not be confirmed dead, Lenin would continue to look for them, causing unrest and weakening his power. Carl and the four other men were each on the same mission, but they were each working alone. None of them knew how the others were operating. They were left to their own initiatives. If they accomplished their mission, each of them would eventually end up at the house where the family was being held. They would recognize each other by their mere presence there.

It was after midnight when the group came together; nobody said a word. They moved on the house, checking every room. There was no one there. Not a trace. The men knew that Czar Nicholas, his wife, four daughters, a son, their physician, a maid, and the dog should all be there. There was no one. The house was in disarray. They knew they were too late, by only a matter of hours. Food was still present in the kitchen.

  The men were despondent about their failed mission, and more so about the death of the innocent children. Carl had been compelled to check the house again. The others would wait outside. Carl searched every room, looking for clues. Did they pack up? Just leave in a hurry, or were they taken by force? Were they alive or dead? By the time he had gotten to the door, he had surmised that great force had been used. Nothing was taken. All of the physician's medical supplies were still there. He would never have left them. When Carl started to leave, he remembered the cellar. One of the other men had searched it when they had arrived. He descended the stairs, moving slowly, checking everything. For a man his size, keeping quiet has an art all its own. As he reached the bottom of the stairs, he could see bloodstains on the floor. He had not used a light in the cellar. The light came from above. Instinct had warned him to keep very quiet and cautious. He stood still for a very long time. For Carl, under these circumstances, it was an eternity. (This is my favorite part of the story. For you should know me by now. I have a soft heart.) There was a sound. Carl had to listen very keenly. Then it came again, a soft rustle, then even more faint, a soft sound of breathing. It almost could not be heard. He had to decide where it was coming from. He stood still for another five minutes or so. He could not pinpoint the location of the soft breathing. He then heard a movement. He located, to his left, boxes. They were stacked, not many, and not very big. Whatever was there was small. He had thought, an animal of some kind. Making his way slowly and quietly,

The Journal

he had moved the boxes quickly. There crouched in a small ball, scared, with the most enormous eyes, was a child, a little girl. Carl had crouched down on his knees and spoken softly to her. Reaching out his hand, he had smiled, telling her everything was going to be all right. He kept saying, "Friend." He was not sure if she could speak English or not. After some time, he had decided that the best thing to do was to let her decide to come to him. He knew that something terrible had happened there and that she was hurt, as well. He knew his size must be very intimidating for a child in her state, so he let her think awhile. He knelt farther down. Then he opened his arms and beckoned to her. She rose slowly and walked into his arms. Carl said he had never been so moved in all his life. All the pain, worry, and uncertainty he had gone through were gone. Ever since he began working with the government, he knew he had been making his way to this moment in time. God had a plan for him. Not just his country, God would oversee it all. She laid her head down on his shoulder. He spoke softly and rubbed her gently on the back to soften her fear. She put her arms around his neck and wrapped her little legs about his waist, holding on with all the strength she had.

    Carl entered the kitchen. There he put together some provisions. As he was about to go up the stairs, one of the men with his group emerged through the door. He was surprised to see Carl with a child. Carl had cautioned him to talk softly. He whispered to Carl that they had found the bodies of the czar and his family. They had been burned. Carl and he surmised that the child he was holding must be the youngest daughter. The czar had four daughters, one being still a child. The

135

man asked what he would do with her. Carl had said, "Get her out of Russia." At the man's puzzled look, Carl answered, "I do not know how, but God will show me how as I go along." The other man replied, "You know, we are all on our own. We have to get out of here. Each has to get word to our own contact. Sorry, but you are on your own." He turned to leave and stopped, turned again, and said, "Good luck. May God be with you." With this, he disappeared through the door and into the night. Carl never saw any of them again.

He hurried upstairs and found the boy's room. He put together some clothes for the little girl and then went to the physician's room. There he checked her wounds. She had cuts and bruises. There were finger marks about her body, where she had been grabbed, and a large knot on her head. Also, a knife wound in her upper leg muscle and on her left shoulder. She was lucky it had gone under the collarbone, all the way through, just missing the artery in her neck. A few inches over and she would have bled to death. Carl cleaned the wounds and applied medicine and bandages. He wrapped up extra supplies to take with him and changed her clothes. These clothes had belonged to her brother. He had known that, along with four daughters, the Czar had one son.

Carl had come to the conclusion that based on the child's wounds, she had been beaten, stabbed with a bayonet and, when she tried to run, had been flung against the wall. She had either been rendered unconscious or had crawled behind the boxes and was too scared to move. He could tell by her eyes that she had seen and heard her family being massacred. His heart had gone out to this little piece of humanity who had

The Journal

the misfortune of being born into this carnage. He was about to pick her up again when he stopped. Something was not right. He assessed the child's appearance and reached for the physician's shears. Slowly, as not to upset her, he started cutting her hair. He spoke softly, telling her why he was cutting away her beautiful long hair. Placing a small cap up on her head, he smiled as he made his way outside. He knew no one would pay attention to a man holding a small boy, but a beautiful little girl would attract attention. When outside, he stopped and set her down on a stump and began to smear small amounts of dirt upon her face and arms to conceal the bruises, which he knew would be more prominent the next day. He was making her look like a dirty child, rather than one abused. He then followed through with himself, so he would match her. They now looked like father and son who had traveled a long way together. With her being so small, she could easily appear to be sleeping as her carried her, rather than hurt.

Carl never left the safety of the wooded areas. He moved as quickly as he could, never stopping until morning. He guessed they had come some distance in the five hours since leaving Ekaterinburg. He was making his way to the border at Skilka. Once he was in China, he would be in more familiar territory and could move more quickly. He had only stopped to check on the child's wounds and to feed her. They had found some food along the way, not much, but enough to keep them going. He had always let her eat first. Only when she was satisfied would he then eat. She never spoke. She would smile from time to time, a small timid smile and only when he would speak and try to play, tickling gently or rubbing a blade of grass across her nose. Her eyes were so compelling. He always said that one could get lost in them. Carl had wished many times that he could have kept the little girl for his own. He knew, however, that in his present occupation, the uncertainty of the future with a war going on, and no mother for her, this was out of the question.

Carl had wondered, along with the rest of the world, when claims of finding Anastasia were announced. He had searched for and had studied her photos. He was positive, with no doubt, that the little girl he rescued was in fact Anastasia. "Her eyes," he said, "I will never forget those eyes. They looked at me all across Russia and China. Since she could not or would not verbally speak, she spoke through her eyes." The last straw to break his heart came when he had left her with another agent, a female agent in Hong Kong who agreed to take her, along with Carl's information, to her next contact. "All I could see were those eyes." He had tried to tell her this was a nice lady and that she would take care of her. "She did not resist, but I watched as she was carried away by the woman. She was holding out her arms to me, begging with those eyes for me to take her back." Carl had been haunted by those eyes all of his life. This is when he had become obsessed with helping children, in much the same way that I did in the case of Mrs. Walden and her children.

Carl had contacted someone about the little girl; I never knew whom. Years later, when reports appeared throughout the world that Anastasia had not been executed along with the rest of her family, Carl had contacted someone about the little girl he had turned

The Journal

over to an agent in Hong Kong. I never knew who this person was. He said it was best for me not to know. He had let them know that he had seen the reports and that he knew, beyond a doubt, that the little girl he handed over in Hong Kong was Anastasia. A week later, word came that he could not be used to verify her identity, for in doing so it would give away his identity and involvement with the government. At that time, he was not to admit to any activities in Russia because he was still on the list at the State Department. He was listed as inactive, but not terminated.

Terminated. I had not liked that word at all, but Carl had assured me that it only referred to his status as an agent. He was always troubled by the fact that he could not help the girl and put her mind at peace. He had not cared what the world thought, only what Anastasia thought. He was not sure if she was positive of who she was or was searching for answers. Be it positive or negative, everyone should know who they are, was all he would say.

After returning to the States, The Antique Jade, and Quan-Yen, Carl confided all that had happened to his mentor and adopted father. He had been placed inactive for a few months. As Quan-Yen had said, "For body and mind and soul to heal." Quan-Yen had also been moved by Carl's story and was a great source of strength to him. Three months passed before Carl was again called, this time just to move about information as he traveled through China and Japan looking for treasures.

Quan-Yen had, for the first time, confided to Carl the nature of the information that he would be passing along. It concerned a treaty that was being put together by powerful men. Later, Carl and the world found out that the "powerful men" were President Woodrow Wilson of the United States, Prime Minister David Lloyd George of Britain, Premier Georges Clemenceau of France, and Prime Minister Vittorio Orlando of Italy. They were referred to as "The Big Four." The treaty was in fact signed at the Palace of Versailles, near Paris, in June of 1919. This treaty officially ended World War I. This helped Carl immensely after the failure of his previous mission. He was so proud to have been, in a small way, part of helping to end World War I.

I cannot remember if I said this previously or not. Dates and times, I can remember. But little things are much harder. Did I say Carl was involved in many more assignments he could not even tell me about at the time? He shared a few more with me, and I chose not to share with you, for I know he would not want me to. Much of what Carl did dealt with the saving of lives. Carl spent much time in and around Russia, Britain, France, Germany, and the United States. The United States did not want to deal with the Bolshevik government. They refused to pay Russia's debts and favored a worldwide communist revolution. Lenin and his Czechs ruled by terror and force and were unrestricted by any law. He eliminated his enemies just as he had eliminated Czar Nicholas and his family.

Carl had also been a part of trying to rescue and remove from Russia a member of the Social Revolutionary Party, Dora Kaplan. She had shot and wounded Lenin with two bullets as he spoke to workers at a Moscow factory. Lenin recovered in several weeks. She, however, only caused greater trouble for her people. Lenin ordered

The Journal

hundreds of so-called hostages to be executed to discourage other attempts. She was also executed. Carl had stated he did not quite understand why the United States wanted to save her. With Lenin's way of dealing with actions of that nature and unrest, he probably would have killed more than he did. Carl would say that those were trying and troubled times. Whoever stated, "War is hell," knew what they were talking about.

Carl was always appalled and amazed by the effects of war. The peace settlement of World War I created conditions that helped lead to World War II. He would always shake his head and say, "Conflict never solves anything. An open mind and heart are the only way you can settle anything. Compromise, not total domination, is the answer. Most war factors are looking for absolute power. Someone has to be the peacemaker."

Carl had taken part in two more missions before his return home in 1921. The first involved information on the movement of Russian troops that closed in on Warsaw in 1920. The information that was passed by agents, including Carl, help set in motion the decision of the U. S. government to send warships to Danzig, in Poland. With the British support of airmen, the Poles repelled the Russian advance on Warsaw.

Carl's last mission regarded information that led to President Harding signing a peace decree, formally ending the war with Germany and Austria in July 1921. As an act of gratitude to the men who stepped down from their service with the government and went on the inactive list, they were unofficially invited to the White House and given an audience with President Harding. He shook each one's hand and thanked them, one at a time, for their participation in the efforts of the U. S. seeking peace. He had expressed with sadness the need for confidentiality. He wished he could tell the world of their heroism.

    Carl returned to The Antique Jade and spent the rest of that year, until December, with Quan-Yen, his true father, in soul and spirit. There, he returned the favor of years ago, caring for Quan-Yen until his death in November from a long-time heart ailment. Quan-Yen had never confided his health condition to Carl, for he had not wanted him to worry. He had no family and had left everything to Carl. It was a small fortune. Carl had sold the business and found homes for many of the artifacts. He had taken the Ming statue back to China, from where it had been stolen many years ago. This had been one of his finest moments in life, to see the faces of the people and to realize the true importance of one's beliefs.

    Carl had one other mission before he returned to the States. He visited Ekaterinburg, where he had found Anastasia. The farm was still there. It was now an orphanage and had been for a few years. It had been established to take care of the children of the war, since so many were left with no one to care for them. Here Carl made the greatest sacrifice of his life. He gave his monetary fortune to the orphanage, with one stipulation: the money had to be used for the children only. He placed an overseer that he could trust to care for the children's needs. His last act there was to change the name of the orphanage to "Little Anastasia's Home for Children." He said a prayer for her and the children and returned home. I have never been so proud of my Carl as when he told his story. That is when I knew that we were kindred spirits, on the same mission for God and

The Journal

life. We have both cared for the orphanage over the years, and it has been my passion as well since I lost my Carl.

Carl was taken off the inactive list twice more and called to serve his country, in 1940 and 1950. I never knew what the missions were for. We never spoke of that time, for I knew if he could tell me, he would. I never asked.

Carl made a statement to me one evening, not too long before he passed away. We were on the porch watching the sun set over the hills behind Sutters Pond. We had been reminiscing over the years we had spent together and the course our lives had taken. He had made a soft chuckle and said, "How ironic life can be. My father wanted me to run for office and be a big political figure that would rise in office and eventually run for our government's highest office. He hoped one day I would be president with him right on my coattail, basking in the pomp, pageantry, and glory that go with the office. Here I sit on a porch, in Vermont, and no one knows my name or could care less. I was a pawn in a very large chess game of life, helping to change the course of World War I and II. I helped my country and government, met a few influential men, the president of the United States, saved a few lives, and I am only one of a few who know who the real Anastasia is and where she is. My father does not know a thing about it." Carl had taken my hand, gave me a wink and chuckle. "We know, don't we, dear? That is all that matters. What a great life. Memories, yours and mine."

Moon Dancer

Sorry, I keep getting ahead of myself, but some of these memories belong in their place to truly finish the train of thought. I don't want to leave anything out. I may give you a peek at things to come, but then life has a way of doing that also.

Carl and I had been married about two years when we knew for sure that something had to be wrong. We had wanted a child, but we never conceived. We decided to see a specialist in New York. We had made a trip of it and took in some shows. When we had seen the doctor, he was at a loss as to why we had not conceived. It was his evaluation that, since we had not conceived a child in two years, he was 95 percent sure we would not be able to have children. We were devastated. Children were very important to us.

The little girl in Russia had introduced Carl to the service of children, while I had been working for children's rights for the previous two years. On our way home, we had talked about a future without children. Neither of us had liked the prospect. Then Carl said, "Why not combine my contributing to children with yours and open an orphanage? Then, we can have lots of children. You can use your law degree, and part of the secret, it will be there for financial help." I replied, "I think we should not adopt any of the children we care for in our orphanage. This way each child will be treated equally, and we should set a length of time to keep trying to have a child of our own." Carl agreed, and we decided to wait six months before proceeding

The Journal

with the plans to open an orphanage.

Carl and I began to make stronger commitments in our life. He became more familiar with the farm and the lumber operations. I have smiled so many times when I remember how jealous the dogs were of Carl in the beginning. They would just sit and look the other way when he was around. It did not take him long, however, before they were following him everywhere. This was Carl. He attracted everyone to him. Businessmen had confided in him. The farmers always talked over their plans with him. Children were drawn to him like the children in the legend of the Pied Piper of Hamelin. They were fascinated by his size, but never afraid.

In church, children would pile on his lap, as many as he could accommodate. He loved them all. He carried them in his arms, on his shoulders, and under his arms with them screaming and laughing. My heart would literally feel as though it would burst when I would think of him with our children. We waited patiently for ours, but they never came. In the fall of 1923, we saw another specialist in New York. We decided we would consult a doctor one last time to see if anything could be done. Then we would continue with our life together with or without children, and we would accept God's will, whichever it may be. We also wanted to finalize the arrangements for the scholarships that had been anonymously awarded to some of the children of less fortunate families in the area. Carl and I were so proud when a young man from our church, Sammie Martins, came up to us to tell us he had received a full scholarship to the Black Forest Academy for the next four years. He had been so proud that he almost cried when he told us. He

145

told of how he had always wanted to go to college, but his family had not financially been able to send him. He had received a letter from the academy stating that they had scholarships available for anyone who showed good aptitude and a willingness to learn. Candidates also had to have a high grade point average. On receiving names from different schools, they would choose someone who met these qualifications. Sammie met them all. He said to Carl and me, "I will be leaving next week. They even furnish clothes for me to wear, my room, and food. Can you believe that?"

Carl and I had driven home that day with smiles so big they threatened to hurt our faces. He had looked at me and said, "I so love this secret of yours. What a wonderful idea your parents had, just wonderful. They must be able to still see the good they have left behind. Thank you for allowing me to share this with you."

Carl and I had left for New York the beginning of the following week. We had visited the law office, and I introduced Carl to everyone on the staff. We were lucky, for Mr. Wheeler was there. I had not seen him since his help with saving the farm. We had much to talk about, all of us. Carl had impressed them all. I could tell that they were very pleased by my choice of a husband. Mr. Wheeler had cautioned Carl that if he were not good to "our little lady," he would have to take matters into his own hands. Mr. Abrams, the senior partner in the firm, had laughed and said he should like to see them in an altercation. He quickly looked at me and stated, "Not that I want you harmed, Miss Abby, it's just that, with the size of these two being about the same, that would be something." He had laughed and added, "Of course, we

The Journal

should have to watch from a great distance." With that, we had all laughed heartily. It was such a wonderful visit. Business was taken care of. We were brought up to date on the financial state of our company and determined how much we could award over the next year. Carl and I had given them the names that we had put together of people in our area who were in need and what they were in need of, and also names of the ones who were to graduate the next year. They would be able to award the students the scholarships before the end of their senior term. This was so plans could be made by their families.

Carl had spoken to Mr. Abrams and his staff about the orphanage in Russia. He had asked if there was any way they could check into this and also oversee it as part of the secret. Would this work? It was somewhat difficult for Carl to conceal his identity and get information at the same time. The orphanage and its receipts would be added to our quarterly reports. Carl could then stop worrying about the children so much, once they became part of the secret. This fascinated Mr. Abrams, and he wrote down the information of how to contact the orphanage. He said, "I cannot wait to check into this matter." He turned to me, took my hand, and said, "Miss Abigail, your mother and father would be so proud. I am as well. You truly have chosen a mate to match yourself. Both of you have matching hearts. You, I know, will have a charmed life. God bless you, both."

I am afraid the visit with Dr. Harmen, the specialist, did not go as well as our visit to the law office. On our return trip, Carl had taken my hand and smiled. He said, "You know, dear, we are grieving, being filled with sadness at the loss of being able to have children. We have to rethink this. We are already parents. We have an orphanage full of young people who look to us for care. Just two days ago, we had a son come and share with us his delight at being able to go to college. The joy and enthusiasm he brought for us to share. Most parents help only their own birth children, which may be only one or two kids. Others have several they cannot even send to school, let alone college. We cannot birth children, but look at how many you have already had since you were fourteen, and all the ones you and I have had since our marriage. They are ours, Abby. We watch them grow. We share church with them. We revel in their success. We pray and comfort them in their sorrow. The only thing we do not get to do is to tuck them in bed at night. You do, in a spiritual sense. You pray for them, and you ask God to care and watch over them. They need us, Abby. Every community needs someone like you and me. God has a plan. If we were able to have children, we would probably have three to six to love and care for them all their lives. We would get caught up in the church community. You would give up your career to be home with them. We would have a good life." Carl had waited a moment for me to think. Then he had said, "Don't you see, dear? All has been leading to this. How many women are where you are today? How many are as strong as you? Don't you think God has been bringing you to this time and place for a much larger purpose than to give it all up to stay home and raise a family? I think not. I have always known you are destined for great things.

"You have to move on, find your place. We have many children, you and I. Some are not even born yet.

The Journal

We have to be ready for them when they arrive. We have others we need to keep a close watch on." It all fell into place. It took Carl to make me see. I had been too close to see. I was waiting for my life to follow the patterns of others. I had forgotten there are some who have to follow a different path. I looked up at Carl with a smile. He knew I understood. We shared a moment of closeness. He said, "If along the way we have a child, it will be God's will. I think that you and I know we will not. We probably knew already. We were just not accepting it. Now we have plans to make. What do you do when you know you are to have children?" I had laughed and said, "You make a home for them. Well, do we buy an old building or build a new one? What shall we name the home for our little angels?" Carl laughed and said, "You just did—'Little Angels.'"

In January of 1924, we opened the orphanage just outside of Montpelier. We called it "Little Angels." We did not want a clinical name or one that set our children apart from other children. All children are God's little angels.

☆ ☆ ☾ ☆ ☆

Within the first year of opening the orphanage, all was going well. We had established ourselves with proper organization. We had all the papers in order and notified people in our line of endeavor. Attorneys had been consulted. We interviewed many, looking for intelligent, good people to help with adoptions. Doctors who would volunteer their time and skills were found to examine and care for the children. At first, a resident doctor and nurse were not needed. We knew, however, that in time the number of children would grow, making this a necessity. Also, as the number of our children grew, so would our staff.

Had it not been for my background in the field of law and social services, the procedure would have been overwhelming. There was so much to do. The proper agencies were contacted, letting them know we were taking children. Our state of Vermont had such an influx of foreign immigrants looking for work in the granite quarries and dairy farms, on the construction of railroads, and, with automobiles becoming more accessible, on the construction of new roads. The majority were poor and in poor health. The death rate of adults was high in the early 1900s, leaving many children orphaned and in need of care.

All children are special and deserve the best life can offer. Occasionally, a child comes along who is exceptional, even extraordinary. We were doubly blessed to have this happen the Christmas of 1927. The children's names were Gayla and Brandon Tarpen. They were twins and devoted to each other. Gayla was the little mother, while Brandon was quiet and more studious than most boys. Their parents had literally starved to death. They fed their own food to their children.

I shall never forget the day Gayla and Brandon arrived at Little Angels. Mrs. Winter, the representative from the state, ushered them into the office. When I looked up, it was as though I was truly in the presence of angels. They literally glowed. They were precious and so polite. After the formalities were taken care of, I took Gayla and Brandon to Miss Emily who was in charge of the

The Journal

new children. This was two weeks before Christmas. We were busy getting the orphanage ready with decorations and food. The children were preparing to put on a play. All were given parts to play. We tried to use each child where he or she was most gifted. Later on that same evening everyone assembled to practice. We were in the large auditorium; everyone was busy with his or her project, and the noise of the children was great.

Miss Emily was playing "Silent Night" on the piano. Everyone stopped. All was quiet, except for the piano, Gayla, and Brandon. Not only did they look like angels, they sang like angels. Every part of my body was overcome. The adults came together, holding hands, hugging each other. Such were our emotions. All was quiet long after the song ended. Gayla in her quiet voice asked, "Was that the way you wanted us to sing?" Miss Emily went to them and taking their hands she said, "Oh, yes, children, that was beautiful. Wherever did you learn to sing like that?" Gayla struggled with her emotions. She was glad, but there was sadness about her. She held herself up straight and proud, then said, "Our mother sang with us all the time." A strong, profound sadness gripped her with as much pride as a child her age could have. She added, "Mother sings in heaven now." Brandon spoke in his tiny voice, "Yes, she sings for God now." There was not a dry eye in the room. I have never been so moved by a child in all my life before or since. Those two children moved right into my heart that night. Had it not been for the decision both Carl and I had made before opening the orphanage, I would have taken them home with me that very night.

It was our desire to make a difference in many little

lives instead of only a few. That is why we chose to have all of the children be ours. We would find homes for each of them and love and care for them equally. We could only do this if we did not adopt children of our own. This way we could stay focused.

That Christmas was one I was never to forget. Gayla and Brandon were the soul of the Christmas play. Practically everyone turned out to hear them. The following day, Miss Emily asked to speak with me. I motioned for her to have a seat. She said it was about the twins. "I have had them sing every style and type of song I can think of, even opera. They are flawless. Great talent does not come along very often. I feel that Gayla and Brandon are gifted, and this gift needs to be nurtured. They need someone who is financially able to give them the right opportunities." I was in total agreement, but was not sure how to accomplish this, for I believed all my children deserved the best I could do for them. I tried to match them with the proper families. I had not once thought of the financial abilities of the family. I was not sure I wanted to, for I believed that God in His infinite wisdom had a far greater plan than I could begin to derive. For the orphanage to try to meddle in these matters was to doom us to fail. Because I believed that adoption was a matter of the heart, my decision was to let nature take its course. I was later to doubt my decision or my lack of it. I am still not sure which one is the way it happened. I know how confusing this must sound to you, but this is how I was feeling and still feel. How are we to always know of the decisions we make? One can appear wrong now, but later on bring about a wonderful result with us sometimes

The Journal

knowing the outcome and sometimes never knowing.

One month after my conversation with Miss Emily, I was introduced to Mildred Pierce. She was representing a private individual who wanted to adopt not one, but two children. They would prefer a boy and a girl, possibly from the same family. They wanted only two children. They thought this would be the best way, since they would only have to go through the adoption process once.

I was so pleased and immediately thought of Gayla and Brandon. This would easily allow them to stay together. It was rare to find a couple that was willing to take two children. I had to battle the emptiness already taking place in my heart, but I had to put my personal feelings aside and conduct myself in the proper manner.

Mr. White was the lawyer for our orphanage; he had been with me since we had opened it. He was a good man, very trustworthy and knowledgeable. He had taken care of at least twenty adoptions for us, as well as numerous foster care cases. He always placed the children with families he had an instinct about and, sure enough, ten of the foster care cases he handled resulted in adoption. Because I trusted his instinct, I introduced him to Mrs. Pierce. I quietly mentioned to him Gayla and Brandon and left him to the business at hand.

I have spent my life caring for children and being aware of their needs. I have been so proud of all that I have achieved, but I cannot find it easy to forgive myself when I fail. It is not just a minor thing. Each child is a life entrusted to me, a very fragile life. These children have already endured more than they should for ones so young. One just cannot fail. I shall forever grieve for my mistake. I know it was early in the life of the orphanage. I was young and so wanted to make a difference. My youth and enthusiasm led to an error I have had to live with all my life. It was a great teacher for me. I never allowed myself to make the same mistake again.

Mr. White had discussed with Mrs. Pierce exactly what she wanted from the orphanage. She had informed him that she was reposting a young wealthy couple by the name of Gunter and Sara Tate. The Tates wanted to adopt preferably two children from the same family. I was to find out later that Mr. White had also let down his guard. He had allowed Mrs. Pierce to handle the Tate's part of the adoption herself, as their representative. Each time we expected the Tates to accompany Mrs. Pierce to a meeting, and they did not come. Her answer was, "I am sorry, but the Tates have been detained. They asked me to take care of our meeting for today." There were so many excuses; Mr. White and I never thought to question their validity. The reason we did not was that the documents Mrs. Pierce brought to our meetings were always in order; the only thing missing was the Tates. During our last meeting, Mrs. Pierce arrived with another excuse instead of being accompanied by Mr. and Mrs. Tate. She said she was sorry, but there was a death in the family. With Mr. White and me feeling sad for their loss, we never doubted the statement. On January 15, 1928, Mildred Pierce walked out the door with those precious children, and we never saw them again.

We had believed that Gayla and Brandon would be raised by a prominent family here in Montpelier. We failed, however, to check out the adopting family, or even

The Journal

meet them. We did a preliminary background check, but only on the information supplied to us by Mrs. Pierce. She turned out to be a very smooth, well-polished woman who exploited children. She used them for whatever purpose would bring her the most money. I have never again been taken like that by anyone. Those poor children paid a high price for my lesson.

Mrs. Pierce took the twins, along with four other children she had taken in much the same way. We will never truly understand the reasoning behind what she wanted with the children; one never understands madness, does one? Mrs. Pierce had exploited twenty children before the authorities arrested her later that year. Someone had called the authorities and asked them to check out an address. What they found was more than my heart could bear. Those children were living in their own filth and were sick and starving. They were taught to steal and were given to anyone willing to pay for them. I learned all of this through the newspaper. I had sat with it in my hand for some time before I realized Miss Emily was talking to me. I could not speak. I handed her the newspaper and she started to cry. When I took the paper into Mr. White's office, all he said was, "My God in heaven." I knew exactly what he was feeling; we had sent these precious children out the door with her.

I returned to my office and gave the article in the paper a lot of thought; then I contacted Mr. Clemons whose name had been in the article as the person to notify with questions concerning the children. Mr. Clemons was in my office twenty minutes after I notified him that I had information concerning the children. When I asked about the twins, he said, "I am sorry, but there were no twins with the children we picked up from the Fulton Apartments." He had called and had someone ask the oldest child about them. He said they had left two weeks before with a big bald man in a large shiny car. I felt so sick, for I knew what this would mean for the children. Mr. Clemons assured me that everything they possibly could do was being done. They were working now to find them. I had to pull myself back to reality and do what I was committed to do, care for children. I could not let my mistake pull me down to the point of making others. I asked him, "Where are the other children? Are they being cared for?" He said, "They are." There were six. After the twins left, Mrs. Pierce had brought two more back. She never stayed with them; she only stopped by to bring them food, and what she brought was never much. Then she would lock them in and leave. When she used one of them, she took them back to her place and cleaned them up before she sold them or sent them out.

I looked Mr. Clemons straight in the eyes and said, "I know you have stated the children are already being cared for, but I would love to care for the children myself if you feel you can trust me after I made such an error and endangered two children." I shall never forget his answer. He said, "Mrs. Hastings, if you live long enough, you will make mistakes. These are the lessons of life, some of which exact a very high price. The shame would be in lying down in pity and not going on with your purpose in life." He gave my hand a squeeze and then gave me a number to call to arrange for the children to be brought to the orphanage. He promised to check on the background of each child and to also personally oversee the search for the twins. He would contact us when he had information.

Two weeks had passed when Mr. Clemons asked to see Mr. White and me. When we entered the office, he was there with a young man and woman who stood up when we entered. They were Mr. and Mrs. Snowden, from Burlington. They were looking for their son who had disappeared from their home a month ago. They wanted to see the boys that Mr. Clemons had found at Mildred Pierce's agency. My heart began to mend when Toby, the smallest of the boys, started to run down the hall, calling his mother and father. I think each of us had a tear. Mr. Clemons smiled and said, "Now that's why I do what I do. Not all make it home, Mrs. Hastings, but some do. Thank the Lord, some do." I understood what he was saying, and I have tried never to forget.

We found out in the weeks to come that two more of the children, Marsha and Sarah, were also kidnapped. The three other boys had been taken from orphanages in New York, Massachusetts, and Rhode Island. The girls were returned to their parents, but the boys wanted to stay with their new friends and us, so we started legal procedures to have them stay. They did, in fact, stay. Two were adopted within four months to the same family. The new parents had wanted only one child, but did not have the heart to separate the boys, who were only three and four. It was a year later before a middle-age couple, that had never had children, adopted Steve. They wanted an older child because of their age. Steve was twelve and had suffered more mental and physical damage than the other children. I was fortunate to have a very competent staff that gave lots of love and the best of care; Steve had come a long way in twelve months. The couple had been informed of Steve's history and his need for continued therapy. They were sympathetic and did not turn away because of his needs. I was so happy that we had taken care of each one of those unfortunate, beautiful children. I was to remember over and over Mr. Clemons' words, "Not all make it home, but some do. Thank the Lord, some do."

Gayla and Brandon were never found. Mr. Clemons never stopped looking for them. Even after he retired, he still kept looking. He had told me on one of his visits to the orphanage that he had four cases he could not let go of. If at all possible, he would search until God took him home. Even then, if at all possible, he would finish his task from the other side. We had both smiled at this. I had said, "Just do not scare me over to your side in the process." We had shared a moment of two souls both caring for our lost children. They were in fact ours, for we had made them so. In our own ways we both felt we had failed them. Mr. Clemons passed away fifteen years later, having solved only one of his four cases. I went to his funeral. I smiled and looked up and said, "Still working from the other side, I see." On his head stone were his words, "Not all make it home, but some do. Thank the Lord, some do." Mr. Clemons had made it home.

During the time of searching for the twins and living life, I was continuing to grow in my experience with the orphanage. More and more each day, I learned the laws that pertained to working with children and the agencies involved in caring for them. I also learned of needs of not only the children, but of the orphanage as well. I started a journal, which I kept in my office. Every time that something was not working, or when I saw a need, I wrote it down. Even if I came across the need or problem in a magazine article or a newspaper, I would put it in my journal. At the end of the month I sat down and went over every one. By waiting a month I was able to cool any anger or resentment I felt at the time I wrote it down and, consequently, be able to look at it with an open mind and a level head. This ensured me a more accurate account of the situation. I would then write at the bottom only the issues or problems that had a chance of being solved. As time would allow, I would use my degree in law to find a legal way around the problem or to change it. At first this was a way for me to work out my anger toward a system that was fallible. I wanted perfection for my children. From the outside everything looked fine: the orphanage was working; we were caring for our children; we were finding them homes; we had an excellent record; our children were happy and healthy; they had a good educational program. Everything was going well, but the system did not always work; too many children were being left out or neglected. There had to be an answer. I remembered the Abby of seventeen; she had found her answer then, and she could still find her answer.

As time went by, instead of saying, "This can't be changed," I asked, "Should it be changed? Yes, why can't it be changed? There's not a law or legal act for it, so we will get one passed. You are a lawyer, get it passed." My next block was the Senate or Congress. They can get laws passed, but someone has to get the issue in front of them. I went on finding answers. Carl was so supportive

Moon Dancer

through it all; caring for the farm and for me, he was my strength. One night, as we were at our evening meal, I was in an agitated state. I had gotten a copy of new rules and regulations governing orphanages, foster care and adoptions. Some governmental agencies are always changing the things that should stay the same and keeping the things that should be changed.

After sorting through my thoughts, I said to Carl and Minnie, "Farm life is not the way it used to be. We are having a problem placing children in foster care. People have stopped taking the children. We have to find a better way to help families so they will adopt. They have to want our children because they love them, not because they need to put them to work."

Carl had looked at me, then Minnie, and then asked, "Well, Minnie, do you have a solution for our agitated lady?" Minnie answered, "No, Carl, I am afraid I do not." Carl said, "Neither do I," he looked at me and added, "I guess you will have to be the one to find an answer. The only advice I can give you is to get with people who have a passion like you do to find a solution to the problems so that together you can find an answer." He stood up and put his napkin down and said, "So, my dear, I am going to go sit by the fire and go over in my mind just what I have to do to be the husband of a woman in government. Please let Minnie and me know when it is to be. We shall both be sure to vote for you." With this, he turned to Minnie, held out his arm and said, "Shall we sit by the fire, Miss Minnie?" "Well!" I had started to make a comment and stopped. I sat perfectly still for close to an hour, my mind trying to sort through all that was just said.

The Journal

When I entered the drawing room, I sat in my favorite chair and looked at both of them. "I shall do just that." They both smiled and nodded their approval. Not another word was spoken the rest of the evening.

Carl was such a wise man. He knew me far better than anyone, and he helped me see exactly what it was I was really saying and how I, not someone else, could change it. On the night that I won my first election, Carl teased me and said, "Poor Father, he was betting on the wrong horse." We both had a knowing smile. I would have to say the changes for women in those days were good for all of us, with the right to vote and run for office. This made for an exciting and productive time. I had women role models that I greatly admired. President Wilson's wife, Edith, was a great inspiration; she stepped in and was a source of strength. After his stroke, she was criticized for some of her actions, but most strong-willed women are often treated in this manner. Her ability to rise above the criticisms gave me courage to try. I had to try; to fail would not bother me as much as not trying.

☆ ☆ ☾ ☆ ☆

Days move in and out of our lives and are slowly taken for granted. One becomes heaped upon the other, and all significance can become lost, especially as we become older and lose that wonderful gift of memory.

For Carl and me, time had settled around us. Our days developed a sameness of fashion and were not as enthusiastically applauded as in our youth. We had become an older couple of habits. With few diversions, we saw to the running of the orphanage. There were fewer children present now as new reforms and organizations were being used to care for them. I feel good about most of the changes that have taken place over the years, and I am proud to have been a part of those changes. We will put children's programs in good hands and, with the assistance of the secret to back them up, all will be taken care of with the New York office in charge.

The "day of sorrow," as I have come to call it, began as most days that year: Carl with his routine and me with mine. Over time, changes had taken place due to a slight failing in health for both of us. The one thing that continued to be a puzzle to me was that when I was alone to reflect and was caught up in memories, my heart was still full of the same passion of youth and the consuming love I had for Carl, the children, and The Old Place. If by chance I happened to pass a mirror or look down and see the rest of my body, I was always shocked to see a woman of age, for my heart was full of youth. I would always choose to laugh and think a trick was being played on me, but really, on reflecting, I would understand that the real trick would be to grow old in mind as well as body. So I chose to enjoy life and stay away from mirrors.

Carl would rise early, as had been his lifetime habit, to see to the farm. He had, over time, dispensed with most of the operation. He kept only the parts that were necessary for our use and needs of the house. Over the years we sold most of the land. Some, especially the land closest to town, was given to organizations and churches for what Carl and I hoped would aid many in need. In time, the towns and cities had grown, and

The Journal

were spreading more and more into rural areas.

Carl needed a certain amount of responsibilities for mind and body. There were a few good and trusted people still employed by us, some of whom had been lifelong friends. My day was, as so many before, a slow unhurried pace of taking care of myself and breakfast with Minnie. Weather permitting we had taken to having breakfast on the porch, opposite Little Tree. Memories of cherished loved ones and places, both past and present, are essential to a well-ordered life and peace of mind. How important to fill our lives with only these as the years pass. Along with the memories of hardships was the joy we shared triumphing over them. The best knowledge, for me, is that God has been ever present in my life. I could never have endured without my faith. I have often thought of those who choose not to believe and I wonder at their survival. How empty they must be.

I am starting to stray again. I will endeavor to relay my emotions from the day of sorrow, as this is the sole purpose of a journal: to relay feelings, ideas, and events of one's life. Some of my feelings about that day, though, I have yet to face or try to explain to even myself. The day passed in its usual manner. I started to notice a change in me, however, as it wore on to later afternoon. I felt uneasiness in me, but most profound of all, was a feeling of emptiness—a void as if I was not totally filled. It was a feeling I identified as being similar to the feeling I had at the deaths of my parents. Having in time accepted it, I had almost forgotten the emptiness. I found it unsettling and continued to go about as usual, thinking that it surely would pass.

Every day, before sunset, I had taken the habit of

walking to Little Tree. I would talk to my mother and my father, always ending with a prayer. On this particular day, when I opened my eyes I saw two graves under the tree instead of one. I looked in disbelief, as the image of the second grave began to fade. I went down on my knees as the emptiness totally consumed me. In that instant, I knew my Carl was leaving this earth; he was going to be with God. For a moment, everything stopped, and I could hear Carl's voice. It sounded as if he were reading from a page and at the same time his thoughts were mingled with his reading. Time, even though it seemed to stop, moved rather quickly. So many years ago, but I can remember as if it were just now. I knew I was seeing and feeling exactly as he was.

Carl noticed for the first time just how slowly he was going. He was nearing the bluff at Sutters Pond, turning left at the bend of the road. The sun was setting just behind the hills; cows were heading home, slowly moving across the field. Stopping, he decided to sit under a large maple for a while.. Everything was as he remembered from so long ago. Surely, all of this would have changed by now after so many years. He thought how he and I had changed, but somehow had also stayed the same.

Was it possible to turn at one point in a road or path and re-enter time? To reacquaint oneself with what was the right time and place of one's life, possessing knowledge and spirit with a greater appreciation of the things of life? A time that will surround and merge with us making us as one. Can we, by sheer force, will ourselves not to let go? To once again drink from our life when it was like a pitcher, cool and full with the water droplets

The Journal

slowly beading up from the coolness of the crystal? To slide effortlessly down in a motion so subtle that you have to be fully aware, lest you miss it all? Oh, how elusive is fleeting time. Was there a secret? Had he missed it or not recognized it when it was possible to grasp and hold on? There had to be more, a surprise around the bend just out of sight, beckoning to us, to just reach out and touch that ever-elusive time.

So many memories were flooding in. Once he had opened himself up emotionally, he was powerless to stop. He knew he was far too melancholy. Men were not supposed to go this far inside themselves. He knew he had gone too far, but he could not stop now. Possibly this is why some say that the older you get, the wiser you get. You start to muse over your life. As we reach the end, we choose to feel and experience the things we overlooked in the past. Sitting here on the bluff now, in the present, Carl could so clearly see the young man of long ago. Here, looking back over his life, there were so many choices. In his youth, he was excited about those faraway places. He was so cocky and sure that all would be here when he returned. He would have it all, the farm, and the land of many generations. After all, it had been this way for hundreds of years. Because he was an only child, it would all go to him and would wait for his return. He knew that she loved him and that she would wait. He had felt the pull from far off. It had pulled him away with the promise of sameness, to always be here when he chose to return. How conceited and arrogant a young man he had been, to think the world would stop for him, that time would be suspended and that she would give her one life, youth, and love to an absent pompous young man. How vain youth can be!

Now he was a very different person with only the distant memory of the boy of long ago. The fading light was descending behind the hills, so amazing, how clearly he could see his life and the consequences. There was little or no fear then, and what little there was had become overshadowed with excitement. Now he found he was consumed with fear, but it was not forceful at all. It slowly faded into a subtle tightness in his head around his thoughts. He felt a slight shortness of breath and the increase of his heart rate. A film was starting to cover his eyes, and he could hear a soft roar starting in his ears. He caught himself up, in a breath, as he thought of how he had almost missed it all. As he closed his eyes and slipped from this life to the next, he smiled as he realized how life could get switched around. Now it was his turn, in death, to wait for her.

Suddenly, I was back and all felt as it had before, but with one exception. I knew that Carl was gone. In time I was to realize what a wonderful gift God had given me. He had allowed me to be with Carl at his death, to know and understand his feelings. God allowed me to know that Carl had not suffered and that his last thought was to wait for me. To know he will be there when my time comes is the most amazing gift God has ever given me.

I sat on the bench at the base of the tree, as Carl and I had done so many times before, and watched the last rays of the sun slowly pass from view behind the hills at Sutters Pond. I said a silent prayer for him and said that I loved him. We would be together again, when God chose to take me home.

The thought of Carl, alone at Sutters Pond, with night

The Journal

descending made me shiver with dread and a chill like I had never experienced before. I found I was making my way to the barn, where Sam was finishing for the day. I smiled, for Sam and Carl were best friends. They had laughed and worked side by side since the day Carl returned, those long years ago. Sam had grown up here. My family had always employed his family, but we all were friends who were lucky enough to work together. Sam, on seeing me, came to me and asked if I was all right. I assured him I was and asked him to please go to the pond and bring Carl back. He said that of course he would. He motioned to Minnie, who was standing on the porch. I did not tell him Carl was dead.

    The rest of the evening was a haze, some memories I cannot put together. I remember Minnie coming to me and taking me inside. When she had set me by the fire and knelt before me, holding my hand, I said, "Carl has gone, Minnie. He passed away a few minutes ago." I will never forget how she accepted what I said. She never once doubted the validity of my statement. I have vague memories of the rest of that evening. Minnie had called our doctor and friend, William Foster. He was in and out all night seeing to me and taking care of everything for Carl. Minnie has told me since that when Sam returned with Carl, Foster, as we chose to call him, had just arrived. Sam had taken it well, feeling proud to have been the one to find him and care for his last needs on earth. He told Foster that he had found Carl sitting at the base of a tree. He had thought Carl was asleep. When he first saw him sitting there, Carl had a peace about him, a softness about his face like he was smiling.

    We laid my wonderful Carl to rest beside my parents.

Moon Dancer

When everyone had gone and I was standing clutching the iron fence surrounding their graves, a glimpse of the vision I had had a few days before flashed. Now, I was seeing two graves, as I had before, and the reality that this would not fade. All the tomorrows to come would find the same two graves, waiting patiently to be three. There was no fear, just the knowledge that when my time came, they would be there waiting for me.

☆ ☆ ☾ ☆ ☆

Some of the years passed more slowly than others. They were all good years filled with friends and fairly good health. The days that turned into years were, however, always filled with the loss of Carl, for he had become as much a part of me as the five senses God had given me to survive. I had chosen to think of love as the sixth sense. Just as I had with the loss of my parents so long ago, I found a way to survive without him and realize that he was everywhere. He would never leave, always residing in my memories. There were even so many of those that I was to find peace and an acceptance I was able to live with.

Minnie and I continued as we had before, with a working and family relationship. She had always been the sister I never had. Growing up without my family taught me the true meaning of family. The family I chose, not just the birth members of a unit, was one having the bond, caring, and commitment of lives to each other. Minnie was in every sense of the word my sister; she was my friend and sister in Christ.

The Journal

Instead of giving physical birth to a few, I became a mother to many. All of the motherless children I could find and take into my care, I did. As any mother, I provided for them and loved them all. I gave of my time to be with them as much as was possible. The experiences of my life had opened my eyes to the fact that there are those who have no recourse. There are those who would and do take advantage of the less fortunate. It is the duty of those who have had the blessings of God bestowed upon them and have been removed from misfortunes to pass on kind deeds to others. We cannot just stop and take for granted our blessings. If everyone passed on a kind word or deed, how wonderful our world would be.

This is why the law has always been my weapon. I have learned that if and when you fight, you must make a commitment to win. You will then only succeed if you choose your weapons wisely. Words and an educated mind are my weapons of war. I read everything I could find on the subject of children's rights. When I began, those long years ago, the resources were few. Today they are many, thanks to the many people who have cared and fought long and hard to make a difference. There is room for improvement, but then there will always be. As our world evolves, so will its needs.

I would not change my life, even with the hardships and loss. They created a place for me to learn and grow. How else was I to be made aware of the needs of others? Isn't this, after all, why we are here? How shall a person of fortune, sitting in the softness of life, experience only the quality and pleasantry of mind? How shall he think past his delights to the suffering of others when suffering

Moon Dancer

had never passed his way? He shall live in ignorance of the plight of the world. Instead of reacting in anger and indifference, we must strive to make a difference. We must try to change what we can and move on with the lesson learned, not sit and wallow in misfortune and miss this, our only chance at life.

How wonderful to have finally reached the age and place in life that allows me to ramble on and philosophize about my life. To have someone listen to it is the ultimate. Old age allows one—me in point, to actually think someone will read my ramblings and take away with them some knowledge of life. Will you? For, if you do, you will have added one more worth to my life, and for this I thank you.

The eventful phase of my life has passed. Now, I am in the reflective phase. Here, I can see if there is unfinished business and seek to change or finish it. This is why I chose, at the age of ninety-one, to write of my life. What a wonderful way to relive all that has come before, to remember places, people, and events that I had forgotten. Ninety-one years can hold a lot of memories. This is why I have chosen to reflect more elaborately on the high points and touch lightly on the less important ones, for I would need another ninety-one years to fully reflect on them all.

Not much of consequence or importance passed within the first year after Carl's death. I was seventy-six when he passed on. I was not in poor health, but my health was indeed failing. I have been as comfortable as possible for my years. I shall not complain, for there are those less fortunate. We must never forget this. When we feel pity for ourselves, and we shall from time to

The Journal

time, the secret is to pass through it, move on. Do all you can, don't stop, and don't even think you are finished, or you shall be.

Having reached the age of seventy-six, I thought life had offered up all the surprises I was to receive. For after all, what was left but to reflect upon it and mildly participate along the way until the end of my journey? I was wrong, for God had one more very large surprise in store for me. After finding out what it was, I realized that the signs, though subtle, were there, but I had not seen them.

I am sure you have noticed that, in my reflective state, I have chosen to give particular days and times in my life names. This day was to be called "My Great Surprise." Early on in our lives together, Carl and I had taken care of our wills and put our wishes down in writing. We had great responsibilities that had to be cared for, even at our death. Now with Carl gone, my world was changing; my needs had changed. Minnie and I were on the porch for one of our many morning breakfasts, as was our custom. We talked of everything. You would think with as many years as we had been together, we would have run out of things to say, but we never did. I remember well the day, I said, "Minnie, I have been thinking. With Carl gone, I need to make some changes here, as well as in my will. There is more land and outbuildings than we need. We can eliminate everything except what is needed to take care of our immediate needs. We can sell the rest and put the monies in the trust for the children." Minnie answered, "I have been thinking along the same line, with one exception. I have wanted to talk to you about it, but I was waiting for you to come to terms with the loss of Carl and be ready to move on with the next phase of your life." This was so like her, to wait for me, to be patient. I will never be able to thank God enough for my Minnie. My interest was growing, so I asked, "What is your idea?" "You and I have always enjoyed this beautiful old place we live in. We have each seen it grow from a smaller size home to this place of many rooms and memories. We each wander around them day to day and take for granted what we have here. Also, from time to time, we find the vastness a little lonely since Carl has gone." She paused, took a deep breath, and waited for me to prompt her, which I did. "Don't keep me in suspense. What is your idea?" "Well," she said, "A lot of the farms today are doing away with the dairies, and lumber is more regulated today than when we were in full operation. It has been ten years now since you and Carl sold the dairy and lumber parts of the farm. Why don't we do what some of the others are doing in our area? Why not share the beautiful old place with others? We can open a bed and breakfast. Keep it small, allow only a few guests at a time. Keep enough barn space for horses to pull sleighs in winter and wagons in time of thaw, and a few animals to make it interesting for our guests. Have nature trails for horseback riding. We can use some of the monies from the sale of the out-parcels to hire the help we'd need to run the house for guests. By sharing this with others we will not have a chance to get lonely and grow old."

I was in awe. How like Minnie to think of that. I had always shared with others, but never my home, not in this manner. I found I very much liked the idea, for I had always loved this place and wished others had a place like it. What a wonderful way to share. I am starting to

The Journal

ramble again, but I assure you, all of this does lead to the Great Surprise. I asked, "And have you a name for our bed and breakfast?" She looked at me in surprise and with outstretched arms replied, "What else could it be but what we have always called it? `The Old Place.'" I smiled at her wonderfully apt suggestion and leaned over and took her hands. " I love it. I love the idea and the name. Let's do it." She smiled and said, "Let's." That is how The Old Place, as it is today, was born. I sit now and write my journals by a warm fire with the sound of laughter and life all around me. People come from all over to see and experience the place of my life, love, and happiness. I choose to think of them all as sharers of my life. How wonderful to be able to do that.

As Minnie and I prepared to put our plan into action, we had many things to attend to. First of all, we had lawyers to see about the many legalities involved with caring for the public. Then there was the sale of land: what to sell and what to keep. There were also people to hire. We found that, rather than being tired with all of the work, we were excited and able to keep up with the tasks at hand.

I still had the secret on my side. I could count on them for help, as it was needed. Also, they were to know of my financial status. The financial books were to be kept with the office in New York, for, at my death, The Old Place and any needs to maintain it would be their responsibility. This was to continue for as long as Minnie lived. I wanted The Old Place to always be her home, and she was to have anything she wished. Carl and I were in total agreement on this. Minnie had been told long ago about the secret.

Moon Dancer

The great surprise occurred as I was making out my will. I was in my office, a beautiful morning room that always catches the early morning light. My most favorite things are here. Years ago, I liked to stay up late, from time to time, to work on my projects in the office. Carl felt that the night air was too damp for me, so he had a small fireplace added many years ago. I usually worked on papers and briefs, all to benefit the children. The children, that's another reason for my love of this room. Everywhere you look are pictures of the children, from all walks of life and all ages. They all are mine in my heart. They surround me and keep me on my path. They are my reason for life. Life does not choose you. You have to choose it.

I have a small baby grand piano, my secret passion. I would have to say this is the only extravagance Carl ever gave me, except the portrait we had painted in New York. Mother was accomplished at the piano. She had brought one with her from England. It still stands in the large drawing room where we received guests. My mother passed on the love of music and the piano to me. I never stopped playing. When I feel the need to be away or to get in touch with myself, I play. It's such a wonderful release and inspiration. Carl knew of my love of the piano and gave me a baby grand on our thirtieth anniversary. I remember what he said to me when he had taken me upstairs for my surprise. How he got it up there without me knowing will always be a mystery. He never would tell me, saying only "some things should stay a secret. This is one of them."

As I stood in total surprise, he said, "Now you can play day or night. If in the night, you will not have to go

The Journal

down to a dark, cold room. You can play anytime." As he kissed me on the cheek, he smiled and said, "You know how I love to hear you play. Now you can play me off to sleep." This I did, on many occasions. We both had remarked how the piano and mother's old desk, which she had brought from England, complemented each other. With our newer purchases, Carl stopped with a puzzled, reflective look on his face. I asked him what was the matter. He answered, "Do you remember the picture that always sat on top of your mother's piano? Where is it? It would look great on your piano, adding a touch of the old with all the new pictures about." I answered, "That's right. I had forgotten about that picture. I am not sure where it is, but I bet I know who does. I will ask Minnie tomorrow." This I did as we were about, getting breakfast. "Yes," she answered, "It is in the attic. We, your mother and I, had removed several things from the lower rooms to the attic. This way, in a few years they could be brought down and rediscovered." My mother had said it would be like magic. Somehow, I never went to retrieve it. I am not sure now exactly why, I guess we got busy with life.

My mother's words were to come to me as I was about, putting my will in order. I sat at her desk with my papers, deeds, and copies of all our holdings. As I was feeling a little overwhelmed, I sat back, took a deep breath, and looked at the piano. I smiled and rose to go over to play. I looked at the empty space on top and remembered her words, "We will take them to the attic so they can be retrieved again; it will be like magic." For some reason, I had to go find that picture and the other pieces. The magic was the thought that Mother was the last to touch them and I would find and hold them. For some unknown reason I felt the need to be as close to Mother as I possibly could. It does not matter how old you get, you never outgrow your need for your mother.

I went to find Minnie and asked her to take me to where she and Mother had put the picture and pieces from the lower rooms. When I asked, she looked puzzled, then said, "We never got them when you asked the last time, years ago." I answered, "No, I had forgotten until this morning. When I remembered, I do not know why, Minnie, but I feel I have to find them."

When we entered the attic it was cool and dark, but not unpleasant. Minnie put on the lights, which were wall sconces. She adjusted them, and we looked at each other, then smiled. She spoke, "A room full of memories." I answered, "Yes, Minnie, mine and yours. Truly they are ours." She smiled, touched my hand, and said, "You have always made me a part of your life and your memories. I thank you for your love and accepting me into your family." I squeezed her hand and said, "You belonged here from the day you arrived. Let's find Mother's magic." We spent the better part of the afternoon browsing through memories, sharing, telling and retelling, finding every piece she had put away.

The last piece to be found was the picture that had lived on the piano. Minnie had found it. She turned and said, "Is this the one?" I answered, "Yes, I had forgotten how beautiful it was." My mother had said it was a picture of where I was born, in England, the Isle of Man. She said it was a beautiful place. She and father were to take me back to see it when I finished my education. They thought it would be a nice finish to my education,

The Journal

to know and understand where I was born. My father had raised his glass in a toast and said, "Everyone should understand from whence one started so that we can appreciate more the place where we arrive." I never got to go back. "Minnie, I was so busy living my life that some of my plans were overlooked." I smiled as I looked at her and said, "You know, Minnie, I am not sad that I never got to go back, for here is my home, my place. I have arrived. England is only a place from whence I started, as Father had said. I would only have gone because they would have. I have no regrets. I did not need to go searching, for all was here. I am so glad I was not blind to that. All was given to me. Sure, some that was given was taken again, but only the physical, never the spiritual. Wonderful parents were given and taken. A sister I never had was given to me and is still here. Carl was given and taken, only to be given again, and then taken. Children we never had were given in numbers too numerous to count. They were taken by life, which is as it should be. All is as it should be, one phase to the next." Minnie asked, "Any regrets?" I answered, "I was too busy for regrets. How wonderful, to have no time for regrets, only a normal passage of time and events, one leading into the next."

Minnie smiled and said, "What a wonderful way to view life, to just let it be. You have lived a very busy life, and we still have much more to come." I asked, "Minnie, do you truly think there is more?" Oh, yes," she answered, "We have a lot to do, you and I. We have a whole new adventure waiting. We are to be innkeepers. Who would have thought it? Really, at our age!" We both laughed, and I rose from sitting on the floor, saying, "Well, it is time to take these parts of the past and put them where they belong, in our present and in our future." As we gathered the items up in our arms, the picture of England dropped to the floor. Minnie and I both stood in disbelief as the glass separated from the frame and the picture. The glass did not shatter. I stooped and picked up the picture. As I turned it over to put it back in the frame, I noticed an envelope, which had once been taped securely to the picture. It was now coming apart from age. I looked up at Minnie. She said, "Open it." I said, "It is probably one of their love letters, and this looks like a legal paper of some kind." I stared at the letter, then my hands began to tremble, and tears came into my eyes. Minnie took the letter and began to read:

My darling daughter,

If you are now reading this letter, it will be because your father and I are no longer there with you. This was to be the second way of telling you a wonderful story, only if we were not able to tell you ourselves. Our plan was to take you home to England, the place of your birth. We wanted you to see the beauty and tell you a most wondrous story.

Our story began many years ago when your father and I met and fell in love. We courted and in due time were allowed to marry. We were so busy with the wedding preparations. Family and friends, all of our loved ones were sharing in our joy. We planned a wedding for Christmas of 1897. All was going well for us. We were married and made a new life for ourselves on the Isle of Man. What a beautiful place!

The Journal

We grew in our love and looked forward to the children we would eventually have. We made new friends and went to parties and functions, as did most young people of our day. I had made a friend of a very beautiful young woman of my age. She and I were in some manner alike, but did not look alike. We were of the same height and weight. Both of us had dark eyes and lots of dark hair. We were instant friends. She, unlike me, was not married. Her name was Judith Gertrude Davidson. As time moved on, we had become as sisters and were inseparable. The only time we were apart was when your father and I were together. He loved her as a sister, as well. They got along famously, and there was never a thought of jealousy. There was no reason. We so hoped that "Tru," as we lovingly came to call her, would meet someone, fall in love, and marry. By all means we would have to love him, too. We would be lifelong friends, share our families, and be a part of each other's lives. We would sit by a fire in our old age and converse. When I would speak of these things to her, she became quiet and withdrawn. I tried to talk to her but would stop short of prying.

As a year had passed and your father and I had not become with child, we spoke of doctors. We decided to wait a few more months before we would seek advice. Tru had come by to see us and tell us she was going to a finishing school for the better part of a year. Even though we were glad for her to have the opportunity to acquire a fine education, we were devastated to not have her here. We hoped to already be with child, as we felt we were, and we wanted her with us for our happy occasion. She felt as we did, but assured us she had to go and would keep in touch. She also promised she would try to be here with us when the time came for the baby. We found we were with child, but within the month, we lost it. We were devastated, especially after trying for so long. It was almost more than we could take.

As the months wore on, we were to have joy and sorrow. Once again, with the loss of our second pregnancy, we went to doctors who assured us, after examinations, there was no reason for my miscarriages. They were at a loss as to why this was happening. They wanted us to let my body heal fully before we tried again. We went home with heavy hearts, but with hope. Over the next few months I rested and took great care with my health. Later in the summer we received a caller very late on a rainy night. Your father opened the door to a man who was drenched. He said he had a message for Mr. and Mrs. Duffin. They were to come with him, as it was a matter of life and death. Miss Tru had sent him. We dressed quickly and went with him. We were surprised to find that we had not gone far when we pulled into an estate, which I thought had been empty, for a time. He pulled up to the door as close as he could. We ran up to the door, which was quickly opened, and a very plump woman ushered us in. She was quite agitated. "Hurry," she said. "Come with me. Please, hurry." We were taken upstairs

The Journal

and into a dark room with only candles by the bed on either side. As I approached the bed, I was so startled to see Tru lying there. She was so pale, her skin blended with the whiteness of the sheets. Her beautiful long hair was wet and stuck to her skin. Her eyes were the only sign of life in her, for they lit up when your father and I came to her. I went on my knees and took her hand. I asked, "Tru, what is wrong? How long have you been ill? Why didn't you send for us sooner?" Only a faint whisper came from her. The whole of the room came to stillness so that she could be heard. "I am sorry to have deceived you. There was no other way. I had fallen in love with a man who was married. Because his wife had a mental illness, it was impossible for him to leave her. The doctor said she would not live long, for such was her illness. We would wait, for we loved each other enough to do so. If it took several years, then we would be together for the rest of our lives. I found I was with child. We decided to say I was away at school, and then I could stay here at Langaleer until the baby was born. In time, we would pretend to adopt our child, and all would be well." She paused for a moment. "Then, something went wrong. My child is well, but I am bleeding. The doctors cannot stop it. I am dying. I do not have long, and her father cannot help my baby, not now. I do not want her here in this. I asked you here to say good-bye and tell you how much you have meant to me and to ask of you, in the earnestness of our friendship, to take my daughter and raise her as your own; to love and to provide for her and cherish her in my stead, for as you can see, I cannot." As she was speaking, the plump woman came to us with a small bundle and handed it to me. At that very moment, my daughter was born to me. At the look of love she saw on my face, my friend slipped in peace from this life. Your father and I stood for a very long time, holding you and crying. I remembered a quote from the Bible at that very moment: When God closes one door, He opens another. He had taken our dear friend to be with Him and put in our loving care her daughter. As we were to find out, we were never able to have children, but we were able to have a daughter. We wanted you to know your true beginning and the wonderful beautiful soul who gave you life. From that night on, you have never left our arms. Your father and I want you to know what a privilege it is to have a daughter like you. You have put a light in our lives that will never be extinguished in this life or the next. Should we precede you into that next life, I shall tell Tru of you and share all of our stories as we wait patiently for you to join us. Be happy for us all as you learn of your life's beginning, for you know the rest. It has always been happiness. We wish we could have shared this with you as we did your life, but as you are reading this, we were not able to. I know not the age you will be when you find this, or your circumstance. I pray both are well and that you will receive this in humble gratitude

The Journal

for giving and receiving our love. You are our hearts' desire, and you know you were well loved. I want to assure you that Tru loved you very much. She placed you from her arms of love to our arms of love. What more can you ask of a mother? What more can you ask of a daughter? We will wait for you. Enjoy your life and give it meaning, as you gave ours meaning.

Mother and Father

Minnie and I both sat in stunned silence. As the minutes passed, we played the words over in our minds, trying to comprehend all that we had heard. Disbelief turned into a glimpse of the past. Times, now that I could see, small questions that were never asked, reminiscences overheard and never pursued. Contentment had canceled them out. When at last I found my voice, all I could say was, "Mother was right; that picture is magic. It changed everything, but at the same time, it changed nothing. It merely told a story of a child I have never known and an unfortunate woman I never met."

An excitement began to come over me. My eyes grew wide, and as I took a beep breath, I said, "Minnie, I can't believe it. You know what this means? I was adopted. I am an adopted person. I have fought all my life for children of circumstance. It has been my life's passion, and now I find we are one and the same. How wonderful that life can give you an opportunity to give back all that you have embraced. It was not until my old age that I was to comprehend how wonderful, Minnie. Can't you say something?" She leaned her head to one side and said, " If you will stop talking long enough, I will." With that we both laughed for a long while.

I remembered the other paper, opening it to find the adoption papers. Names and signatures, dates and times, my birthdate. The papers were filed one month after my birth. Five months later we came to America and Vermont. I have never left. There was another paper written to me.

> Dear Child,
>
> I am not a man to show or express emotions well, although your mother has shown me much in our time together. I am not sure how to say this. Although I shall never know you, I wanted you to know you were conceived in love. I truly had every intention of marriage to Tru when I was able to do so. Life had given me a challenge and love at the same time. I could not turn my back on my responsibilities, nor could I not love Tru. She was the only thing that held me together. When she passed away, I lost my strength. I know one day I shall return to a form of myself. I just don't know when.
>
> For this reason, I shall allow you to go. I know in my heart that you will be well loved and cared for with the Duffins. This was Tru's wish. She knows me well and that I would not be able to care for you properly at this time in my life. However, I shall love you always in my heart. You will reside there with my Tru. I shall not sign Father, for I am not, even though I wish I could have been.
>
> Claude Faulkner

The Journal

    I felt only sadness for these people of long ago and detached pity for the loss of their lives. How strange to sit here at the age of seventy-six and realize that you were conceived in love and surrounded by such sadness. The time in which this had taken place forced an altogether different ending than it would today. Time, places, and circumstances have such a bearing on the outcome of our lives. I could only feel sadness and compassion for the two people whose love had produced me. I also felt such gratitude for them placing me with my mother and father, for I had been truly loved and cared for. I could not wait to go to Little Tree, as I did every day, to talk to my parents, for today I had much to tell them.

    As Minnie and I made our way to the lower part of the house with our treasures, she asked, "Will you do anything with this, Abby?" I answered, "No, Minnie. Conception was but a moment in time. My life is an eternity in comparison. You cannot find a lost speck in this large world, no point in looking. We each received what we needed in that moment, and I shall always be happy with that. Thank God for His gift of them to me."

    Later, when I was standing under Little Tree, after my talk to my parents, I looked up through the branches. How beautiful it was. I thought of the tree's story, which Father loved to tell, and how empty it would be without it there. What significance it had played in our lives. I spoke to Little Tree, "You know, I just realized you were adopted, too. You and I were brought to this land, loved and cared for to flourish and grow under the watchful eye of two loving people. Now you stand guard, shelter, and protect to return the favor of so long ago. You grew along with us. Now, your very life, force, and heart, which are your roots, will forever hold and cradle them as my father's cloak cradled and sheltered you those long years ago. Some may think me a little mad, talking to a tree. Without the whole of the story and its truth, they would be right."

I made my way back to the porch, ascended the steps, and turned as I leaned on the banister. I looked out over what was and is my life-home and love—how strange that all was still present, still here, but ever so different. All that I loved and cherished, all that had played such a part in my life was all here on this: the west side of my home. My mother, father, Carl, Little Tree, the hill and valley, home of Sutters Pond, the dairy barns and outbuildings, the lumber business and sawmill were all on the one side. My rooms and balcony were above. When I stood there, I could see my entire world just as I always had since I was a child.

At my age, and being alone except for Minnie, I did not feel the need to leave or even a sense of loss at not having ever left. No, I had not seen much of the world, but I had experienced much of what the rest of the world had missed. I felt content, no real regrets, no unanswered dreams. Even my travels had been far and full of adventure, for Carl had taken me so many places on long quiet evenings by the fire. He had shared his adventures with me and told them in such a way that I truly felt I was there. I knew I felt everything almost as much as he had. Even, over the years, when he was called back to go on a mission, he eventually shared the stories with me. Sometimes he would go as long as ten years before he was called upon to do a mission. They continued to use him because he was someone no one would suspect.

The Journal

The last time he was called, he was fifty-six years old. So you see, through Carl's stories, I traveled, saw the world, and had excitement. I have written all of Carl's stories down, and from time to time, I read and re-read them. They keep him alive, and I relive the memories of those long evenings together. He had the gift of telling a story so that it put you there. When you are snowed in, in the Vermont winter, this can change long spells of solitude.

I am sorry my mind has started to wander once again. Let's see, where was I? Oh, yes, on the porch. Later Minnie and I had a light supper by the fire in our favorite room, the one we called the drawing room. She asked how I was feeling after the events of the day. I assured her I was fine. I had reflected on the events of my life and in fact was pleased with how it had turned out. Learning about my beginnings and adoption, at my age now and without my parents, was as it should be. Nothing in me had changed. All was as it should be. All was in place. I had just been told a story of a small child and the unfortunate circumstances of her life. How love, compassion, devotion, and friendship were the keys that opened a new and wondrous world for the child. I patted Minnie's hand and said, "I do so love a story with a happy ending." Minnie smiled. We both rocked and sipped our tea, both of us lost in our own thoughts.

The next few years found us in the throes of being innkeepers. We learned through trial and error over time. We worked out the best way to run the business and still have time to keep our personal lives. We managed to find good people to help us run the place. We changed some things about the farm to make it more interesting for our guests and found that it put back a purpose and fulfillment.

Moon Dancer

We reopened the dairy on a much smaller scale. We had our own process for preserving milk installed. The milk we serve comes from the cow to the table, which our guests find fascinating. Also, we leased the old lumber mill to a very fine man, David Brenner, and his family. He was a wonderful wood carver and maker of fine furniture. He opens his doors to the public, and our guests enjoy watching him create a work of art from a piece of wood.

The gardens about the house provide an abundance of fresh produce. The leftover produce is canned and stored in wonderful large old pantries for our winter guests who wish to weather the snow and beauty of the rugged outdoors. The pantries are a source for fine stews, soups, and great hearty meals at the close of the day.

Since opening The Old Place to the public, Minnie and I have met and shared our lives with many new friends. We have been so busy that we have not noticed time passing so quickly. I have just of late noticed my age and now know that my time is at hand. No, do not feel remorse for me, for I am now ninety-one with a very long and fulfilled life behind me. I believe God, in His infinite wisdom, gives us insight and expectance to know when our time is near. Peace has come over me lately. I do not feel frightened at the awareness that I am to leave this life. I know I am to go on to my next life. I wait with anticipation.

Strangely, as my body grows weak, my mind grows stronger, enabling me to withstand the pain of my body. I feel it is really my soul being born. The pain is merely the contractions of my body as it prepares to push forth my soul into its next life of freedom, to be with our Father, our Lord God and His Son, Jesus Christ.

The Journal

How special I feel knowing where I am about to go.

I know that this is the night I shall be taken to the hospital, when I finish my writings. I sit here by the fire in my favorite room, with the shadows playing about. How strange my feelings, for I know I shall never again do this. I shall never again return to all that I have known and loved here. Ninety-one years is such a long time. So many lives I have experienced, so many women I have been. We have to move from one to the other. I feel that the hardest thing for a woman to learn is to love herself for all the women she will be in a lifetime, and at ninety-one, I have been many.

I find I see more now in these last few moments than I have before. Part of me does not want to let go, for this is the familiar. At least here I know who I am. Even though I feel I know where I am about to go, I—my human self—is finding it hard to let go, while my spiritual self, my soul, is ready to be free. There will be peace when I finally go. My mind is so full. All of the corners are filled, each memory struggling to be heard, each saying, "Remember me". I hear the sounds of the house. All is being readied for the holidays to come and the guests that are to arrive for Christmas. This will be my last Christmas, but I shall not be here for it. I shall be in the hospital, preparing for my journey home. If I could have but one request, one last gift that God and life could bestow on me, it would be to spend one last Christmas, free from the pain in my poor old body, here in this beautiful Old Place. To see it, experience it, and relive the wonderful old memories and make some new ones.

I shall be content in my memories today, for I know tomorrow I shall not remember.

Judy— the Christmas Surprise

I sat with tears streaming down my face. I could not control them and would not even try. I had never been so overwhelmed and moved. I was spent. It was as if I too had lived ninety-one years in a matter of hours. How alive everything around me had become, now that I understood. I laid the journal down in its place on the nightstand by the bed and lovingly caressed the soft pale leather. I spoke out loud as if she were there, "I know I probably should not have read your journal. Thank you for writing it. I so enjoyed your story."

Moving about the room, all of it now had meaning—the pictures of the children and the piano. I now knew how much she had loved it, and she did in fact play beautifully. I held my head slightly to one side, and if I listened intently, I could hear the faint notes of nonexistent music mingled with the crackle of the fire from the adjoining room. When I opened my eyes, it was then that I saw the picture of the English countryside in its place on the piano. I gently touched it, remembering the story behind it. I wondered if indeed, everything was there in the frame. I them smiled and thought, where else? That was its home, exactly where it belongs. How right everything was. I was, for the first time in such a long time, at peace. I silently closed the door to Miss Abigail's room and made my way back to mine. I did so with an overwhelming sense of wonder and awe. I should have been feeling shame for invading her privacy, but I did not. How incredible to have lived the life she had, with one all-consuming love, and how rare to have found it at such an early age. I marveled at the strength and faith it took to wait for him: waiting for him to wander the world, grow to become a man, develop his character, realize the force of his love for her, then return a complete man with high morals making him a true mate, partner, and lover to her for fifty-six years. These were the thoughts I took with me as I climbed into bed. Smiling, I snuggled, pulling the blankets up under my chin and drifted off to sleep.

The chimes woke me as the clock struck three, but I had the feeling that there was something else that had woke me. I listened for a few minutes, hearing nothing. I was about to drift off to sleep again when I heard another sound. I checked the secret door, but it was closed. I got up and went to the window and looked out. There in the snow was Buck running and playing with the two dogs. A soft light was coming from the doorway of the barn, throwing back a glimmering gold off the snow. What was he doing at this time of the night, playing in the snow? Why do I feel this tightness in my stomach whenever I see him? I realized that I knew and suspected that I had known all along. I just

Judy—the Christmas Surprise

did not want to face the truth. The last time I had loved, I had lost him. Dealing with his death had been the most pain I had ever had to endure. I do not ever want to go through that again. I climbed back into bed and willed myself back to sleep.

Soft shadows danced about on the walls as the fire slowly burned down. Buck crept into the room by way of the secret door. His shadow was added to the many shadows already there. His eyes were only on the sleeping form before him. She was so beautiful, with a childlike innocence. He knew she was closer to his age than being a child. He had a feeling she chose not to grow up, to stay in that place somewhere between reality and dreams; this only added to her beauty. It gave her a searching quality, as though she were waiting for something. He could feel the pounding of his heart; he placed his hand upon his chest and took a deep breath to calm himself. He was a big man and had never been afraid to take on anything life had to offer, whether it be a difficult task or another man. So he was a little puzzled at the fear coming over him at the thought of what he was about to do. Would she scream, be afraid, or, even worse, laugh at him for showing his softer side? The thought of not ever knowing scared him even more. With the decision made, Buck reached out and gently touched Judy's shoulder.

I woke with a strange feeling, not scared, but knowing something was about to happen. The room was different; the air felt charged with energy. I sat up and saw Buck sitting on the foot of the bed with the biggest smile on his face. He said, "You sure are a sleepy head. I was not sure how to wake you. Can't have you screaming and waking up the house, now can we?" "Is something

Moon Dancer

wrong?" I asked. He replied, "No, it's Christmas morning and time for you to receive your first present." He placed a stack of clothes beside me, got up, and turned away, saying, "Now get dressed and bundle up really good. It's still a cold night." "Where are we going?" I asked as I started to dress. "It's a surprise, " was his answer. I suddenly came to a stop as I realized what I was doing. Here was a man I hardly knew in my room at four in the morning waiting for me to dress to take me outside for a Christmas surprise. *Am I crazy?* I thought to myself. I would never consider this. I immediately answered myself, "No, you wouldn't, but this new lady would; the one I have become since arriving here, the one who has grown to like and trust Buck. More importantly, the one who is developing feelings for him." Now I am going over the edge. I am having a conversation, a lucid one, with myself while dressing in the same room with a man at four in the morning and going off, God knows where, with him. I think I am getting better. I knew the answer should be the opposite, but in the same instant knew that the truth, the real truth, was yes. The right thing to do was just what I was doing.

Dressed and with myself settled, I walked up behind him and softly said, "I am ready." As Buck turned around and looked down at me, everything came to a stop. The world, my breathing, the fire, everything was, for a moment, suspended. I could only see into the depths of his eyes. I felt there was only infinity there, a place I could go and never come back, more importantly, never want to come back. Just as suddenly as I had lost myself in his eyes, I was jolted once again back to reality, when he reached out his hand and mine got lost in his. As he

Judy—the Christmas Surprise

led me to the secret passageway, the door swung silently open and he disappeared inside, taking me with him. The door closed and everything closed in around us, for such was his size.

I found that I was laughing a soft, gentle sound. "Won't you get stuck in here?" He smiled and said, "Not so far. I hold my breath all the way down, on an exhale, rather than an inhale." This he did, looking much like a little boy. I was laughing so, I could hardly move along. Being aware, I had to stay as quiet as possible.

Buck led me down the winding stairs, lighted only at each landing by the soft glow from a wall sconce. I realized he had made a right turn rather than going straight down to the kitchen. I had not been this way before with Miss Minnie. It grew darker, and the air became stale with a strange scent to it that I was unable to recognize. It was just out of my mind's reach. *I should know this, but I cannot place it,* I thought.

Suddenly, we entered the vastness of a large empty room. It had not been used for some time. Large windows let in a muted gray light from outside. There was a soft whistling sound, as the wind moved gently over the panes. "Where are we?" I asked. He answered, "The old wing of the house, the one that burned many years ago when Miss Abigail was a little girl. They rebuilt most of it but left this part the same for storage." A cold chill came over me. I could feel panic coming over me, a need to get out. I found myself saying out loud, "Smoke. That's the smell. I was not sure but it's smoke." Buck could sense the panic coming over me and led me quickly to the door and out into the cold night air. He watched as I slowly began to calm down and lose the look of wild panic.

Moon Dancer

"What happened?" he asked. "Are you all right?" I was not sure, myself, what had happened. I answered, "Miss Minnie told me the story about the fire and how it affected Miss Abigail. I guess I was seeing and remembering it through the story. I'm sorry." "No, that's OK. I am just glad you are all right. You had me scared for a moment." At this moment the dogs chose to make their appearance, nearly knocking us both down. They were very large dogs of the shepherd breed, often found on farms throughout Vermont.

With the friendly attack, we were once again brought back to reality and the cold. The wind, although it was not strong, was blowing about the soft flakes that lay upon the ground. It made it look like it was snowing, yet it had stopped before midnight. Buck reached down and effortlessly swept me up into his arms and closed the distance to the sleigh, which he had waiting for us. "How beautiful the Morgan, as black as midnight," I said out loud. Buck answered, "Roman is his name. He is a beauty, and I would trust my life to him—and have in many storms." Buck wrapped the blankets around my feet. I could feel the warm bricks he had placed for heat. He ran to the barn to put away the dogs and close the door. A strange feeling came over me, and I looked up at the window on the third floor. I could just make out who I thought to be Miss Minnie. I laughed to myself. "Now don't tell me, you are going to take credit for this." As Buck climbed in and placed the blankets around us, he asked, "What were you laughing at?" I answered, "Oh, I was just looking for a card." At his puzzled look, I laughed again as Roman moved off into the night. The night changed as we moved further away from the farm.

Judy—the Christmas Surprise

The stillness was present everywhere; the only sound was the sleigh. As it slid effortlessly over the snow, you could not even hear Roman as he trotted ahead of the sleigh. The further into the forest we moved, the brighter the stars in the sky and the more the moon shone down upon the snow. All was changed; everywhere was magic. The beauty could take one's breath away. I slowly allowed myself to be alone with the rhythm of the world around me. I could feel my senses become more alert and in tune with those about me: Roman, his pace, and his muscles ripping with his efforts. I could feel his strength and sureness. I somehow knew that this is what he liked and where he belonged, out here in the wilderness, master of his world. This man beside me, I knew, was so like his Morgan: a proud man, strong and sure of himself, but with a gentleness to move quietly and not overwhelm his surroundings, to blend in harmony with the rightness of the world. I somehow knew that we both were aware that all things have a time, and place, and purpose. This was ours. No headlong whirlwind, no loudness of this space, nothing shattered, no need for a grand entrance, just a powerful bonding of two souls. Only God could change that. I also felt that God was placing His blessings all about for us to see. When you ever, at one time or another, say to yourself, "Would God be pleased," just pay close attention to the answers around you. All you need to do is look and listen, for He can be heard only in the quiet stillness of the soul. When you slow down, everything about you can become as one with Him. This is not where He lives. We have to go to Him. We tend, over time, to get caught up in the modern world and forget

Moon Dancer

our way, but the soul has not forgotten its way back to God and never will.

As I listened, Buck's breathing was so soothing. I could feel his heart beating as I sat next to him, and I could see the muscles in his hands as he held the reins. We began to slow for a turn. There was a slope ahead. We slowly approached the top and came to rest on its summit. I gasped as my breath was taken away by what was before me, for I had never seen a more beautiful sight. The snow sloped down to a frozen pond. The moon caught upon the surface and twinkled, thrown back in a profusion of tiny lights. All the trees were heavy with snow, which reflected again the little lights. Behind the pond was the town with all of its Christmas lights. They, in turn, twinkled their colors as an accompaniment and magical backdrop for God's beauty in the moon and lake.

As I looked in awe, I turned to Buck and he said, "Merry Christmas." "I cannot believe it. I never knew such beauty existed," was my answer. He spoke softly, "It is always there. It is just waiting for us to slow down and look for it. I have waited my whole life for the beauty I see in your soul. I always knew you existed. You were somewhere just out of my sight, just out of my reach. I had to slow down enough to recognize you when you passed. You cannot see or feel someone's soul when you are looking with your eyes and feeling with your body. These things are for later, after you recognize the person who is like you, on the way to a grander life than earth has to offer."

I was suspended. There with his words all around me, for the first time, I realized that what he was offering me had no beginning and no end. Like God's love,

Judy—the Christmas Surprise

it had always existed and always would. If I never saw him again after tonight, if something happened to either of us, we would go on, we would still exist, for true love of the soul would endure and live on inside us even when our earthly selves ceased to exist. Buck placed his hand upon my cheek and spoke softly as he looked into my eyes. "I love as love was meant to be. I have a wonderful peace about me. It arrived the day you came up to me and spoke. Your words went past me. I can no longer remember them, but your presence never left. It moved in and took its place where it belonged. It filled the emptiness inside me. Thank you for becoming a part of my life here on earth. I know we will be together again, at the end of our earthly journey." I placed my hand over his and said, "I was so frightened by my life experiences that I almost failed to recognize you. I tried to reject my feelings, but the peace and sureness you possess helped to ease my fears and slow me down enough to see all around me." Buck kissed me softly. I could feel the dampness of his tears as they touched my cheek. Our tears ran together as he took me in his arms, pulling me across his chest. He held me for a long time. No more words were needed. Just to be together, to enjoy the night was all we needed. I found myself thinking of what most men would say of the previous events; they would not understand this wonderful big man having the courage to listen to his soul and express his feelings. Most men are afraid to open up in this manner. They are satisfied to have meaningless relationships rather than a lasting love, and, I am sorry to say, a lot of women are becoming that way too. Thank You, God, for not letting it be too late for us.

Moon Dancer

The sleigh was positioned sideway to the view of the valley, pond, and town. Buck poured a cup of hot chocolate and turned his back to the opposite side of the sleigh. He placed me in front of him. (Yes, when a man as big as Buck is moving you, "placing" is the right word.) I leaned back against him as we enjoyed the serenity and drank our hot chocolate. I felt so safe and loved, cradled there with the whole expanse of him around me. We talked of everything, including his life with a dominating father who meant well, but got lost in his ideas of family and responsibilities. He told of a woman, some years ago, who had been very important in his life. She had helped him keep a sense of the right and wrong of his ways when they were very young. It was not a love relationship, just a loving and bonding of two young people who were kindred souls. He had moved away and not seen her for some time. Then he said, "I have never been in love before, Judy. I will only be with the woman that I love. Will you be my forever love?" I was so moved that I had started to cry. He wiped my tears away. I turned to look at him as I spoke softly, "You know I was married. My husband died some time ago." He smiled, placed his hand upon my cheek, and said, "I can see you loved him very much. This is good. It makes me happy to know you were cared for and loved. You understand about a loving relationship. This is what I want for us. I will always love you, care for and watch over you." I said, "I am afraid I will wake in the morning to find all of this a wonderful dream. A dream had by a lady on a Christmas holiday, in a beautiful old home on a hill, full of memories, searching for her lost love of so long ago." I leaned over and gently kissed his cheek and

Judy—the Christmas Surprise

said softly, "You are too real to be a dream." He laughed and said, "If it is a dream, then we both shall never wake. We will make it an endless dream, and each day we shall design a new one to lock them together eternally." Laughing, we kissed again, a soft warm kiss of promise for more tomorrows.

The skies began to change. They became grayer as morning tried to break its way in over our world. Small animals began to move about, and the wind began to move softly, stirring up the soft powder of the fresh snow. This wonderland had moved in and taken over me. I knew its beauty and the miracle that had taken place on this beautiful Christmas morning would forever affect me. As we made ready to return to The Old Place, I placed my hand on his, and he turned with reins in hand. I smiled at him and said, "This has been the best Christmas present anyone has ever given me. Thank you." He leaned over and kissed the tip of my nose and said, "You are most welcome, my love." With this he tugged at the reins, and Roman began his return home. I had to turn and look back, just once more. I wanted the picture forever sealed in my mind. Roman trotted more vigorously now than when we came out. "Do horses get cold?" I asked. Buck let out a hearty laugh and asked, "Hey, Roman, do you ever get cold?" With this asked, Roman let out a very high-pitched whinny, and we both started to laugh as we went gliding over the snow with the bells jingling. This had to be a dream. Please don't let me wake.

We pulled up to the barn. All was still and quiet. It seemed to be more dark here than out in the open. Buck said, "I'll take you up and then come back to put Roman and the sleigh in the barn." I put out my hand to stop him and said, "No, I would like to help." "OK," was his answer. When we had finished, we ran from the barn to the kitchen. I said a silent thank you to him for not taking me through that old, smoky room.

We quietly entered the kitchen. No one was about. The embers had burnt down to a soft glow. Buck picked up a large log and placed it in the grate. He stirred up the embers, and we watched as the log began to burn. He stomped the remaining snow from his boots and warmed his hands. He reached for me, gathered me in his arms, and just rocked me back and forth. How pleasant this was. Finally he said, "We all have much to do today. I had better get you to your room." He took my hand and led me to the stairs. I said, "I can go up alone. You need to go." "Excuse me, Miss, but when I abduct a lady from her boudoir, I always return her to the same." With this, he gave a very wide bow and curtsy, which, for him to do, was so funny. Up we went. I again marveled at how he could fit through these tiny stairwells. When we reached the landing, he pressed the sconce and the door opened without a sound. He said, "The lady of the bell tower has been safely returned." He gathered me into him arms and kissed me passionately. "I love you and always will." He touched my chin with his fingers. "I will see you in a little while," and then he disappeared down the dark corridor of The Old Place.

Christmas Morning at The Old Place

When I entered the room, I was with mixed feelings, one of being overwhelmed and also one of disbelief. Taking the fire log poker, I stirred the ashes about and added a log to the now smoldering fire. I sat on the edge of the small couch watching the flames grow, wondering if I would suddenly wake to find this all a dream. Did I in fact want it to be so, or was I ready for life once more, both the negative and positive? If this, with Buck, had taken place before I had read the journal, I was sure I would have a different perspective. The story of Miss Abigail's life gave me a calm acceptance of my life now. Can a person pass their demeanor on to another, just by sharing their life story with them? No, I was not just taking up her beliefs. I was realizing that her life is as God had intended all along. I was merely using it as a design. Buck was the first step, that of trust.

The clock chimed the six o'clock hour. I realized that Buck and I had been gone for two hours. The house would soon begin to stir. A big breakfast was planned, and presents were to be opened by the fire as stories of Christmas past were shared. There were those who would be off to church, visiting friends, or just relaxing by the fire. I would hopefully be off to visit the orphanage and hospital. I was anticipating meeting Miss Abigail. Miss Minnie had planned to spend the entire day there, and I hoped to join her. If I did not get dressed and go downstairs, I would do neither.

I descended the stairs to the front area and dining room; to the right I could hear the cheerful laughter of the other guests. It came to me that I had used these stairs only twice since my arrival. I laughed to myself when I thought, *I know more about the back and secret part of the house than I do about the rest of it.*

Everyone was dressed in their finest for the occasion, complete with corsages. I had chosen from my limited wardrobe what I thought was a smart red and black pantsuit. I had bought it because it was wool. I would need it for warmth and easiness for the ride into town. The room was aglow with candles and the large open-hearth fireplace. Presents were placed beautifully under the tree, decorated in the theme of children and animals. It was then I realized that the presents were for the children at the orphanage. Our gifts were exchanged, food was eaten, there was lots of conversation, questions were asked, but no one waited for an answer; they just moved on to the next one. At one point in all of this wonderful chaos, Miss Minnie and I caught each other's eye and laughed. She shrugged her shoulders, stood, and began clearing away the dishes. I also took a tray of food and dishes. She held the kitchen door with her back for me to enter. We both laughed as we spoke of the revelry

Christmas Morning at The Old Place

going on in the dining room. "Well, they are certainly having a grand time," she said. I agreed. She had asked if I was ready to leave in about an hour. I had said I was. I had asked if she was going to the orphanage with me. She had patted my hand and said, "I think you should go there alone. It is a very soulful experience. I will have Buck take me on to the hospital when we take you to the orphanage. He will then come back for the others and take them on to church. When you finish your visit, you can walk the five blocks to the hospital." She saw the look on my face and asked, "What is wrong?" I answered, "Are you sure it will be all right for me to see her?" She replied, "Yes, please come. Even if she does not wake, you can see her. Now run along and get your things. I will see you in a little while."

I was standing by the counter where we had placed the dishes. The Waters sisters had thanked me and hurried about their task. They were to go home to their families when the morning chores were finished. I was about to return to the others when I remembered there was something I had wanted to do ever since I read the journal. I wanted to visit Little Tree. I slipped out back, through the kitchen door. The coat and boots I borrowed from the rack by the fireplace were a little big, but warm and comfortable. I found my way around the outside of the house and past the side of the barn. It was then I remembered that it was the huge tree I had seen on the day I arrived. I approached and stopped in my tracks. How beautiful it was. Even in its winter undress, it rose higher than the house and stretched almost as wide. I could imagine it in summer and fall with its profusion of colored leaves. What a wonderful place. As I came to

Moon Dancer

stand at the foot of the graves, a smile played upon my lips when I recalled how Miss Abigail chose not to separate her parents. To let them, in death, continue to be as they were in life: side by side, together for always.

Now after experiencing the miracle of the night before, I was able to understand and appreciate the love they had for each other. How fortunate for them to have a daughter who was able, at such a young age, to see and understand this. Her beloved Carl was there resting beside them, the three great loves of her life waiting for her to join them. There was a place prepared for her beside Carl. I said a silent prayer for them. A wife and daughter were now so close to being reunited with them. What a wondrous thought. For the first time, I was at peace. There was an acceptance of the soon coming passing of this. Their child, Carl's wife, the mother of so many children that had benefited from knowing her, a friend and benefactor to so very many was finally coming home. I thought of her other favorite place. I looked toward the pond. I could not see it, but I knew it was there just under the snow. I could imagine how it must look during the other seasons. Life and the earth, each has its season: spring to be born; summer for our youth, to run madly through life; fall for us to begin to change, eliminating old ideals and discovering life; winter for us to prepare for sleep, to see the beauty in the sleeping season, to rest for a while, only to awaken again in a new life.

I had been walking and thinking and now found I was standing on the slope that led down to the little valley that cradled Miss Abigail's pond. I was remembering how she referred to it as her church. Looking out over it

Christmas Morning at The Old Place

I said aloud, "I wish you could see it just one more time, for it is not merely a church, but a cathedral in endless white beauty, with a little sun peeking through playing upon the ice." I could see and understand her feelings for this place, the lovely old home, Little Tree, the many memories of her loved ones, the expanse of the vista all around and this special place, which has cared for her throughout all the seasons of her life. How fortunate for her to have found happiness for an entire lifetime in one place. To be content, to have it all here and to have the wisdom to recognize it comes from the heart and cannot be found in the world: so very wonderful. I stood for some time absorbing all that was around me, realizing some would think me a little unstable, but there would be those who would understand so well.

When I returned from my visit to Little Tree, I freshened up and went to meet Miss Minnie. I stood on the porch and watched as Buck bundled her up nicely against the cold. They were so sweet together, this giant of a man with the playfulness of a little boy, beside this tiny little woman with the inner strength of an army. How perfectly they fit. You could see they absolutely adored each other. This gave me such peace. I was so glad I had given in and made this trip. I shivered at the thought that I had almost changed my mind. The depression and overwhelming desire to hide, not to emerge into the light of the world, were almost a memory now. I thanked God for giving me this gift. I would not have missed it for the world.

The Ride to the Orphanage

As I walked to the sleigh, Buck looked up and gave me a big smile and asked how my morning was. "Miss Minnie has been telling me of some of the wonderful conversations going on inside." I replied, "They are wild, but having a great time. You will need a tranquilizer when you return to take them to church." He laughed and said, "Why don't I just give them the tranquilizer, since I am driving?" I laughed and replied, "Good idea." As he walked me around the sleigh, he said, "I saw you at the Little Tree this morning. I am not sure why, but I just can't bring myself to go there. I have tried several times, but I just can't." I then replied, "I found peace there, a reason for this place, another piece of this tapestry called life—Miss Abigail's life." He then replied, "That was why you were in the attic the day I came looking for you." "Yes," I answered. "I was so intrigued. Miss Minnie took me there. She let me explore my way through the past. It helped me to reconnect by reaffirming my faith. I was also able to recognize you." His smile and wink was not lost on Miss Minnie.

Moon Dancer

Buck bundled me up as he had Miss Minnie and we were off. The morning was beautiful. I loved it. The sun was not heavy, just a gleam here and there on the snow, just enough to make it interesting. As we took off at a leisurely pace, we traveled the trails rather than the roads. Miss Minnie smiled and said, "Our Buck here knows every trail there is and can travel them with his eyes shut." She turned and gave me a knowing smile and said, "I am sure you found that out last night or, rather, very early this morning." I laughed and said, "I thought that was you at the window." She waved her hand and said, "Now, dear, I just heard a noise." I told her Buck had taken me to see the pond and the Christmas lights of town from the hill. She gave me a knowing look as she said, "And I suppose afterward he took Miss Maria and Miss Nancy as well." We both broke into laughter. Buck turned and asked, "What is going on back there? Let me in on the joke." We both said, "You were," and then went into a fit of giggles again. "Women," he exclaimed. He shook his head and gave his attention once again to the reins.

It was so strange to be in a town, riding in a sleigh. It really was like a childhood fantasy all come true and wrapped in a beautiful package. We wound down one street and another. The Christmas lights were so beautiful. Christmas was everywhere. Then we pulled up in front of this lovely old building that was decorated for the season. Miss Minnie patted my knee as she said, "This is where you get out, my dear, Miss Abigail's orphanage." Buck jumped down to help me out. I was amazed. "It doesn't look like an orphanage. It looks like a large home." "That, my dear, is how it is supposed to

The Ride to the Orphanage

look. Miss Abby wanted a home for her children, and this is it. She always referred to them as God's little angels. This is how the name came about; we refer to it as 'Little Angels.' You have a wonderful visit. I called Mr. White, who takes care of the place for Miss Abby. He has a title, but everyone has, by now, forgotten it. Everyone knows this place would not be the same without him." "Thank you, Miss Minnie. I will see you in a little while. Have a good visit with Miss Abigail. I pray you find her well." She replied, "Thank you, dear." Buck helped me over the curb onto the sidewalk, gave me a soft kiss on the cheek, smiled, and said, "Have a good day, my love. I will be waiting for you at the hospital to take you home." I smiled and said, "Thank you. This has already been such a special day."

I stood and watched until they were out of sight. I just could not take my eyes away. How really strange and wonderful everything was. Now, I was going to get to meet the children, her children. I could hardly contain myself. I took a deep breath and walked up the walkway, stopping to read a very small plaque: God's Little Angels Orphanage—founded and established by Mr. and Mrs. Carl B. Hastings, 1924.

God's Little Angels

The orphanage was such a nice place. It was on the edge of town, which the mountains almost encircled, and was surrounded with many beautiful evergreens. This time of the year was when they were dressed in their finest, with snow on their branches and beautiful birds for a little color. I could just make out the playground area to the side and back of the main building even though it was partially covered with snow. The place had been around for a long time; my guess was 1870 or so. This only added to its character. Someone had taken very good care of this place. Their attention to detail produced the feeling of home. They accomplished a cozy atmosphere without destroying the character of the building. There were three stories to the building, these being much higher than modern ones. There were other buildings of varying sizes off to each side. It was very impressive. I liked the original color, a dark burgundy blended with the dark red of the bricks. A modern trim and shutters the color of medium beige had been used to soften the effect, a wonderful blend of today without losing the feel of yesterday.

When I entered the front door I found a very cozy, comfortable room. There was a large, but not crowded, seating area. A beautiful Christmas tree stood in front of the one very large window overlooking the street. A large number of plaques hung on the walls displaying all kinds of awards won by the children over the years. There were comment letters from state and government officials praising the orphanage for its success. It had achieved the state's highest award. I'm sure Carl and Abigail would have been so proud of these accolades.

When I turned, there on the wall was the very same picture that hung in Carl and Abigail's bedroom the large portrait over the fireplace and mantle. If it had not been for the Christmas tree, it would be the most prominent feature in the room. I now understood why they had wanted someone who could capture their love for each other. Nothing else would do, not here among their children. There were two smaller plaques, one on either side of the portrait. On closer examination I saw that they were both poems written by Miss Abigail. They were about her devotion to her children. Tears came to my eyes as I read them.

The Misplaced Child

> The multitude of faces
> By circumstance have lost their place
> I will gather them to my breast
> And find love for them all
> None are bad, not a bad one do I see
> Just lost children struggling to be free

God's Little Angels

Free from hunger, free from pain
Free from the cold, not to sleep out in the rain
A roof, a bed, a place to be fed
A mother's love, to show them their way
I must give to my children their place
Surround them with warm hearts and lots of love
Give me strength, dear God,
In all that I do
To my task at hand
I thank You.

All Belong to Me

My children of the future and the past
Surround my children of the present
They consume my time
And fill my space
Remove my sorrow
Erase, leaving not a trace
How can anything in my life
Be more than the life of a child
With no sense of worth
No mother or father's love
My pain becomes mild
Compared to the needs of a child
To me none were born
But all were entrusted.

The poems were a tribute to the children who, through no fault of their own, find themselves in a world with no place to belong and no family to care for them.

Moon Dancer

A door, behind me and to the left, opened and brought me back to the present. When I turned, standing before me was a beautiful little girl, about eight years old. She was dressed in her Christmas best. She wore a dark-green velvet dress with red and black velvet ribbons and a matching ribbon in her strawberry-blonde hair. She said, "My name is Sara. Are you Miss Judy?" I said, "Yes, I am. It is so nice to meet you, Sara." She was very excited, and it took a lot of effort for her to stay calm. Looking up to me with her eyes aglow, she said, "I saw you when you came up in the sleigh. I have always wanted to ride in a sleigh. The horse is beautiful. Will they come back for you?" I bent down on one knee and said, "I am so sorry, Sara, but I am to walk to the hospital to visit a very nice lady after my visit here." She said a little sadly, "That's OK." She quickly changed back to being happy. "Mr. White sent me to bring you to the dining hall." I asked, "Are you eating Christmas dinner?"

"No, we are making it, and you get to help," she replied.

Sara grabbed me by the hand, and off we went down the hall and out a back door. We crossed the snow-covered play area and entered one of the buildings I had seen when I arrived. The dining hall was a very large room full of confusion because everyone was laughing and talking at the same time. On one side, women were preparing food for the Christmas meal. There were children stringing popcorn and making cookies. In the middle of the room the tables were set for the meal to come. The far end of the room was set aside for the Christmas presentation.

A man approached me and introduced himself as Mr.

God's Little Angels

White. He was pushing forward a young boy, who had been hiding behind him, and saying, "This young man is Brad. He and Sara are inseparable." The next two hours passed with much excitement and lots of food. The auditorium was the perfect place for a large gathering. I was remembering the Christmas Abby wrote about in her journal, what a magical night that must have been. The children brought me back to the present. They went to the stage and sat in front of it where the Christmas tree was. It had been decorated with handmade ornaments, and strings of popcorn and cranberries were wound around the branches. There were many presents under the tree all wrapped in brightly colored paper.

☆ ☆ ☾ ☆ ☆

The guests for the presentation began to arrive and take their seats on comfortable sofas and overstuffed chairs. The entire half of that end of the auditorium was made to resemble a living room. There was also a variety of holiday print pillows scattered about the floor for the children to sit on, leaving the furniture for the adults. The room even had its own baby grand piano, just like the one in Miss Abigail's morning room. I had just finished my thoughts when a young girl in her teens sat down and began to play softly. Mr. White walked to the front and, with a smile on his face, said, "I'm sure most of you know, by now, the story of the first Christmas the twins arrived here at the orphanage in 1927. My father never grew tired of its telling, although it is in fact a sad story. We have chosen to celebrate it as a wonderful life

Moon Dancer

lesson teaching us to always appreciate those around us and never to forget to say 'I love you' or 'You matter to me.' We don't know what the future holds. So, today we remember two beautiful children, Gayla and Brandon, orphans who have a mother in spirit in Miss Abigail Hastings, a segregate mother who devoted her life to finding homes and parents for all who were entrusted to her. Unfortunately she did not for Gayla and Brandon, whom she loved very much. Gayla and Brandon were twins who disappeared in 1928 and were never found, but we will never forget them. Audra will play the piano; Sara and Brad will sing "Silent Night."

Sara and Brad smiled at me with much excitement as they left my side to stand by the piano. I was so surprised and moved by this tribute to Miss Abigail and her missing children. When the children began to sing, I found myself transported back to another night so very long ago; Gayla and Brandon would be so proud to have these children portray them. There wasn't a sound, not even from the other children. My heart seemed to stop in my chest. I had never heard such beautiful voices coming from children. I too wanted to call them angels, just as Miss Abigail had so long ago.

The ladies stopped clearing away the remains of the meal, for they were transfixed by the children's voices. When they began to sing "Ave Maria," it was as though a spell had come over us like magic. The magic of Christmas. I couldn't but think of baby Jesus, God's gift to the world. We were now hearing His gift through the voices of these beautiful children. We must never forget the children of the world and how very precious they are.

When the song ended, the room was silent. No one

God's Little Angels

moved for a very long minute. I didn't realize I had risen and gone to them until I knelt down, touched their faces, and gave each a kiss on the cheek. I said, "How beautifully you sing. You sound like angels." They answered at the same time, "Thank you, Miss Judy." Then Sara touched my face and said, "It is you, Miss Judy. You are beautiful. Thank you for being here and for all you have done. We know that you love us; we love you, too, and will never forget you." The spell was broken when everyone came to praise Sara and Brad. The room then became filled with even more excitement as the gifts were exchanged. I had brought a gift for Elizabeth, the name I had chosen from the Christmas tree in the parlor.

   I sat and watched the joy of the children and couldn't help thinking how I wished Miss Abigail could be here. She should be the one here instead of me. I found myself talking to her as I had done so many times since coming here. "You should be here; you did a wonderful thing establishing this place and caring for these children. I have never seen this kind of devotion. Most people today have grown used to instant results; not many could wait as long as you for results. I must be honest with you, Miss Abigail; I feel very small next to you. I must rethink my life. I won't try your ideas; I can find my own way. I haven't looked into my soul for some time. I will have to start there." Looking around, I had to say once again, "You did a very good thing here, Miss Abigail, a very good thing."

   The morning and early afternoon passed all too quickly. I knew it was time to go. I had so enjoyed this day, meeting Mr. White and learning more about his father who had been the lawyer for the orphanage since

Moon Dancer

it opened. Unfortunately he had passed away five years earlier. Then there were the children, especially Sara and Brad; how will I be able to say good-bye to them? I said my good-byes to everyone. When I approached Sara and Brad, I could see they knew I was leaving. There was something special between us; it may be that we would never be able to put a name to it. After all, some things are just meant to be accepted as they are and nothing more. I held each of them for a few minutes and said, "I will see if I can come back tomorrow with the sleigh and take you for a ride. Would you like that?" They both started to smile and became excited, saying, "Yes, could we please, with that big horse?" I said I would come for them tomorrow. I then followed the path across the playground to the sidewalk in front of the building. I took a deep breath to gather my thoughts. When I began to walk in the direction of the hospital, I could hear someone calling me. I turned to see Sara and Brad running toward me. I went down on my knees, and both ran into my arms. We stayed just so, for a few minutes. They both said, "We love you," turned, and ran back to the building. They turned and waved smiling, and then disappeared inside. Walking away, I was still trying to put a name to what had happened today, but it was just outside my comprehension.

The Church

I walked away from the orphanage with a sense of wonder. How had I lived my life up to now, oblivious to the plight of others? When had I become so caught up in myself? I had moved out of the world. I suddenly realized I had been walking without knowing where I was. I then noticed a magnificent old church across the street. It was very ornate with a bell tower of majestic height, topped with an immense cross. One could tell by the patterns of design and its weathered appearance that it had been here for many generations. The stained glass windows caught the sunlight, producing a prism effect. Since I was not Catholic, I did not know if there would be an evening mass for Christmas or just a morning mass. There was no one about; it was unthinkable for me not to go inside.

When I entered, it was even colder than it had been on the outside. The cold seemed to totally surround me and go to the bone. It was then I noticed the burning candles by the altar. I was drawn to them, their flames promising warmth, which I could feel beginning to come over me. Standing there before the altar, visions of the children began to fill my mind. How easy it had been for me, in the past, to get caught up in myself. I felt such shame as I thought of the plight of all those children, past as well as present. I struggled to replace the shame with this new feeling of rightness, one of coming home to myself. I thought, *What a strange way of expressing this new feeling,* but I knew it was the proper way. It is possible to get lost from one's self, to go away from one's ideals. How wonderful now to feel alive again. As I sat on the first pew, I saw before me the statues of Christ, the Madonna, and the Christ Child. My joy began to overflow, and I spoke aloud, "Dear Lord, how appropriate for me to feel reborn on the day we celebrate the birth of Your Son, Jesus Christ. How wonderful to spend the morning in the presence of those lovely children. Lord, I had but one morning with your small ones and found myself so moved. Miss Abigail has had an entire lifetime caring for them—how special she is! I pray for her now, dear Lord. Give her peace and ease as she passes from this life to the next. I am not sure how it is to be there, but I feel a sense of rightness when I think of Carl waiting for her. This is as it should be. I believe we will know each other in heaven. After my husband passed away, I stopped loving. I thought there would be no other, but then you brought Buck and me together. You gave me love again. Thank You, Lord, for all my blessings, and thank You for all of Miss Abigail's. Please send another for the children now that it is time for her to go."

Leaving the church, I gave in to the impulse to visit the cemetery. Walking among those who had passed on

The Church

confirmed my own mortality. For the first time, I wasn't afraid. I knew now that when my time came, I could go. I stopped and stretched out my arms, saying out loud, "All these souls, Lord, it is as though I can feel them. I am not afraid." I gave a small laugh and looked up and said, "I am not crazy. Am I, Lord?" Others would likely think so, as I would have before I changed, before coming to this place and meeting these wonderful people and getting caught up in their lives. One life is leaving us, and my life is being given back to me.

Flashes of all that had taken place since boarding the plane filled my mind. I had never felt more alive than at this moment. How ironic to be experiencing my rebirth while standing in a cemetery. At that moment Revelation 21:4 came to me: "And God shall wipe away all tears from their eyes; and there shall be no more death, neither sorrow, nor crying, neither shall there be any more pain: for the former things are passed away." What better place than in a cemetery to feel the power of God and understand the finality of death and the ultimate joy and wonder of rebirth into what will be our afterlife, here where the bodies of departed souls are laid to rest, being of no more use. Their bodies have served their purpose. They are merely a facility for learning, for beautifying the soul on its journey back to the power of God. Statues of angels, crosses, and Jesus Christ were all about. They are signs of what those who had passed, as well as those who are waiting, believe of our journey and its end. These are the symbols of the reality of where we came from and where we are to return. Our soul is aware, even if our earthly self has forgotten. It was evident to me as I looked around that

Moon Dancer

humanity had not forgotten. It was then I noticed a headstone with the name of Samuel Clemons; below was inscribed, "Not all make it home, but some do." I thought he too understood. How appropriate.

The large evergreens were heavy with snow, and snow was lightly dusted over the beautiful granite headstones and statues. The presence of a single cardinal was the only color added to the white and slate grayness of the cemetery: red for Christmas, Christmas for the birth of Christ, and the cemetery for birth of a soul.

I became aware of voices and movement as others visited departed loved ones. The world was continuing on and had not noticed that a life had been given back to a lost soul. I remembered a quote I had once heard and liked very much, quite fitting for this moment: "Things and their placement are irrelevant to the passage of time." *How true*, I thought as I closed the gate to the resting place of those who, in death, surely understood now its true meaning.

I continued my walk to the hospital, thinking that I was about to intrude where I did not belong, but I had to go. I knew in my heart that if I turned away now, I would regret that decision for the rest of my life.

The hospital was smaller than I had envisioned, but then land and space were all I had really seen since arriving. What a beautiful state. I could not wait for Buck to show me every inch of it. Opening the door and entering the lobby, I was to experience a strange sensation. I could find no name for it. I just added it to the many since my arrival here.

Poinsettias were everywhere, and Christmas decorations were placed about beautifully. A very large

The Church

Christmas tree, decorated with old-fashioned ornaments of every shape and size, filled the lobby. Strings upon strings of berries and popcorn were lovingly placed. The tree was topped with a beautiful angel made of old-fashioned lace. In a sense, it was as if the holiday season and the atmosphere and meaning of a hospital were in complete contradiction. Standing there looking at the angel, I was reminded of the promise and God's gift of His Son; therein lay death with the promise of new life. In this sense they were so very much alike.

Not many people were about; those that were, were laden with packages and flowers. Dressed in their festive best, they added rich color to an otherwise drab interior. With smiles upon their faces, it seemed they had chosen to favor the pleasant side, that of healing and going home. I guess in a way that is what Miss Abigail was about to do.

A very young, pretty girl attended the information desk. She was wearing a headset and listening to music; she was in a world of her own. I guess if you are not a part of what someone else is experiencing, you can look a little ridiculous. I surely hoped no one had been watching me recently. When I leaned over to her, she pushed back the headset and with a big smile said, "Can I help you?" I answered, "Yes. Can you please give me the room number for Miss Abigail Hastings?" She checked her chart and replied, "Room 239, second floor."

"Do you know how she is today?" I asked.

She answered, "When you get to the second floor, there will be a nurses' station. They will be able to answer your question." I thanked her and found the elevator. As I was standing there waiting, the feeling that

Moon Dancer

had no name returned. On the way up, it grew stronger. I wasn't scared; I just could not explain it.

There were two nurses standing at the station chatting quietly. When I approached, one of them walked away. The other one smiled and asked if she could help. I answered, "Yes, I am here to see Mrs. Hastings. How is she today?" She answered, "Resting very comfortably. She had a good night. Miss Minnie is with her now. Do you know Miss Minnie?" I answered, "Yes, I am staying at The Old Place for the holidays. I hope you will allow me to see Miss Abigail. Miss Minnie thought it would be all right for me to pay a visit." She said, "Of course, but not for long. She is in a weakened state and does not need too much excitement." The other nurse had returned as we were speaking and had heard part of our conversation. She was excited as she said, "I just love that old place. I have always wanted to go there, even as a little girl. I am not sure why I never did. It is so beautiful, especially at this time of the year." I added, "Yes, it is. I fell in love with the place the moment I saw it and your wonderful little town. I felt as though I was coming home." They were both smiling as I talked about my sleigh ride in to town this morning and the marvelous old buildings. As I started to leave, I said, "The first place I visited this morning was the orphanage—what a beautiful place for the children. Miss Abigail certainly has done a splendid job of keeping the place like a home. I loved every one of the children. You just want to take them all home with you.

"There was a Christmas tree at The Old Place, and each of the guests drew a name. My child's name was Elizabeth. She loved the gift I had gotten for her and

The Church

asked me to come back after my visit here. Thank you so much. I will visit Miss Abigail now. I hope to see you both later. If I should miss you, have a merry Christmas." When I turned to go, I had not seen the two women look at each other with a questioning face. The younger of the two said, "What orphanage? I didn't know we had an orphanage in town!" The older lady looking at me as I paused with my hand on the door said, "We don't anymore; it was moved to Burlington some years back. Miss Abigail had become too frail to actively participate. There is only a very large, empty building there now."

I placed my hand on the door and slowly opened it; I was excited and apprehensive, for I so wanted to meet her. I prayed that she would still be with us and in good spirits. After all, this was Christmas. Surely, God would give her the gift of Christmas once more. When I entered, she was lying still upon her bed with her eyes closed. I thought I had never experienced a quiet as this before, such a great lady, to be so frail. She had moved the world with her mind and her will. Now she waited for her ease. She gave over to the frailty of her body and a life lived fully. How can I do this, invade her privacy? These are her last days, and they could be only hours, precious hours. She would want to spend them with Miss Minnie. I reminded myself that while she did not know me, I knew her through her journal and her friends. I can't go, turn around and walk away. I knew in my heart that all that had passed before was leading me to this moment. It was a deep understanding, a certainty. I had to be here to say good-bye to her, but most of all to thank her for the inspiration she had indirectly given me. I had to share with her how she had helped to restore my mental state, as well as my spiritual.

There would be those who would never know her or of her death, but I instinctively knew that mankind would. Her essence would be present for all time. Goodness would always exist. I knew in that moment that the spirit lived on, in and around us, trying to mend fractures in the core of our being, to heal pain, sickness, loneliness, and help restore lost souls to God. I had no idea how long I had been standing there, or just when I had entered the room. I realized I was standing at the foot of the bed with my hands gripping the rails. The energy could be felt in the room; it was as though it could be heard crackling as it arced about. Slowly, some form of reality began to take shape. The room and its contents were clear to me. How strong our emotions can be. I was so overwhelmed that I had no memory of my entering the room and taking hold of this bed.

Miss Minnie was sitting by Abigail's bedside; our eyes met, and I started to speak. It was then that I noticed a soft glowing light. Miss Minnie put out her hand to silence me. When she rose from her chair, a calm peace came over me. I now knew the answer to all the questions I had about Miss Minnie's ability to anticipate my needs. How had I missed the answer? Surely I could have seen, but I knew in my heart why. I had been looking with my earthly self and not with my soul. Getting to know this great lady had shown me my way back to God. Now my soul was open. God in His mercy had restored to me knowledge of the spirit. I saw before me an angel that I instinctively knew to be Miss Abigail's guardian angel.

I said, "I did not recognize you. How blind I have

The Church

become. You have come for her to take her home, but why have you appeared to me?" She answered, "I am here for you too, Judy, as well as Miss Abigail. I have always been here for you. It has been my privilege to care for and watch over you since the day you were born. There were times when you knew I was there and times when you had forgotten. This is the way of earthbound souls. You choose to be born in human form, bringing your spirit or soul, as you know it. As a child, you remember and understand. When you grow, your free will comes into being. With the gift of human life, God also gives us free will to learn the lessons of life. God becomes real to some, while others choose to forget. There are those who make a difference, who touch others and change lives along the way." I was so overwhelmed that I could barely speak, but I managed to say; "Miss Abigail certainly did all of that, and even now when she is close to death, she has changed my life."

The angel placed her palms up and extended them out toward me and calmly spoke, "I was speaking of you, my dear. I am your Guardian Angel." I started to shake, and tears rolled down my cheeks. I said, "How can this be? I am no one. I have not mattered. I have been weak, grieved for my losses, forgotten my blessings. I did not make the world a better place." The angel spoke, "Don't judge yourself so. God has seen and heard. He has always been present. He has been there every time you were in crises. You asked for Him, and He was there. When you saw hunger, evil, injustice, any need, and you asked His help, He was there. God has answered all your prayers, in His time, for the good of all. You waited for your prayers to be answered, and never losing faith, you endured hardships that came while you were waiting. You, my dear, never lost sight of God while you devoted your life to others. God understands that as a human you have limitations. He expects no more than you are capable of. He is a true and just God, and He is so very proud of you. God's words are written in the Bible, and they are for you. 'Well done, my good and faithful servant.'"

I sank to my knees. I was so humbled by the presence of this angel and her message. I was becoming powerless to control my emotions. I slowly gained enough composure to raise my head and look at the angel. I asked, "Is it my time? You said, 'Well done,' as in the finish. I cannot see these achievements in my life." I pulled myself up and looked to Miss Abigail and said, "This lady is all that you have described. She has always lived for God. I am no one, in her presence and God's. Can't I stay and use the lessons I have learned? God has shown me that even though I loved deeply once, I could love again. Life recommences, and we must use every precious moment and not waste it on regrets and idleness. I do not mean to question you or God, but why would He give me an understanding of life, a plan for His love, and the ability to feel so strongly all that is around and within me? Why would He give me a true man of God who will always be beside me? Why give me all before I am to die?"

The glow of the room became more intense and the energy more pronounced. The angel I had grown to love as Miss Minnie smiled the most radiant smile. Her very presence was awash in radiance. There was love flowing from her to me. She opened her arms and replied, "A gift, my dear child, an amend for your faith and devotion through the tribulations of life. God is so proud of the

The Church

beauty of your soul." I became aware of another presence and turned to see Buck. He was holding Miss Abigail's hand. His eyes were kind, and I could see to their depths. There was an answer, and I knew that he understood. In a voice I did not recognize as my own, I asked, "When did you arrive? Can you see the angel?" He smiled and answered, "Yes, I see her, and I have been here all along. I have always been here with you and loved you since the day we first met."

My mind could not comprehend what they both understood. I said faintly, "I do not understand." The angel replied, "God answered your prayer, your last request. He chose to answer in such a way as to allow you to see and experience your life in a unique way. You, on the night you came to the hospital, as you finished your journal, stated in its closing, 'If I could have but one request, one last gift that God and life could bestow on me, it would be to spend one last Christmas free from the pain of my poor old body, here in this beautiful Old Place, to see it, experience it, and relive wonderful old memories, and make some new ones.'

"To make it possible to answer your request, God held in His keeping a large part of your memory. He left enough for you to become a complete new life. God gave you the greatest gift of all, the ability to see yourself as others see you. While your body lay in repose, your spirit walked among angels that God sent to watch and guide you on your journey of enlightenment. Do you now understand the depth of love God has for you and all who willingly choose to serve Him? You, my dear, are Judith Abigail Hastings. God has sent your one true love, Carlton Buckley Hastings, to guide you on your

Moon Dancer

final transition, from this mortal existence to your next existence as a soul, a spirit of life. You will connect with God's radiance and accomplish your lifelong dream, to become as you have always referred to yourself, 'a Moon Dancer,' one of God's rays of light."

Miss Minnie took her hand and helped her onto the bed. She lay down and opened her eyes to see Carl, as she remembered him from so long ago, and Minnie, who had been a wonderful companion and friend. She looked upward and said, "Thank You, God, for all of my blessings, but most of all, I thank you for loving a poor mortal who in this life could but try."

☆ ☆ ☾ ☆ ☆

> So when this corruptible shall have put on incorruption, and this mortal shall have put on immortality, then shall be brought to pass the saying that is written, Death is swallowed up in victory.
>
> —1 Corinthians 15:54

Follow the characters of *Moon Dancer* in Patrilla Elliott's next two novels, *Shadows of Me* and *Faded Glory*.

Shadows of Me

Elaina Cook, Angle Walker, and Falon Drescher try to expose a past so bizarre and twisted that it is unimaginable, and in the process they reveal the real reason for the disappearance of the twins, Gayla and Brandon. Caught in the darker edges of life where reality and shadows overlap, these three women emerge into God's light and truth.

Faded Glory

Carl Hastings—secretive, courageous, and humble—was also fallible. He knew he had long ago been forgiven for his moment of weakness, but he never knew its effect on the world. *Faded Glory* takes you on a journey of fulfillment, softening the edges of life, and bringing you to a place of realization that God is in control.

☆ ☆ *To Contact the Author* ☆ ☆
E-mail: PatrillaElliott@aol.com